THIS DIARY BELONGS TO:

Nikki J. Maxwell

PRIVATE & CONFIDENTIAL

If found, please return to ME for REWARD!

(NO SNOOPING ALLOWED!!!☹)

MacKenzie Hollister
is taking over!

ALSO BY
Rachel Renée Russell

Rachel Renée Russell

DORK
diaries

Drama Queen

with Nikki Russell and Erin Russell

SIMON AND SCHUSTER

First published in Great Britain in 2015 by Simon and Schuster UK Ltd
A CBS COMPANY

First published in the USA in 2015 as Dork Diaries 9: Tales from
a Not-So-Dorky Drama Queen by Aladdin, an imprint of
Simon & Schuster Children's Publishing Division.

Copyright © 2015 Rachel Renée Russell
Series design by Lisa Vega
The text of this book was set in Skippy Sharp and Beautiful Every Time

1 3 5 7 9 10 8 6 4 2

Simon & Schuster UK Ltd
1st Floor, 222 Gray's Inn Road
London WC1X 8HB

Simon & Schuster Australia, Sydney
Simon & Schuster India, New Delhi

A CIP catalogue record for this book
is available from the British Library.

HB ISBN: 978-1-4711-1770-1
Export PB ISBN: 978-1-4711-1771-8
eBook ISBN: 978-1-4711-1772-5

Printed and bound by CPI Group (UK) Ltd, Croydon, CR0 4YY

www.simonandschuster.co.uk
www.simonandschuster.com.au

www.dorkdiaries.co.uk

MIX
Paper from
responsible sources
FSC® C020471

Simon & Schuster UK Ltd are committed to sourcing paper
that is made from wood grown in sustainable forests and supports the Forest
Stewardship Council, the leading international forest certification organisation.
Our books displaying the FSC logo are printed on FSC certified paper.

With love to my twin brothers,
Ronald and Donald

Thank you for being
the inspiration for (and
the subject of) the very first
book I wrote as an aspiring
author in fifth grade!

ACKNOWLEDGMENTS

A special thanks to Liesa Abrams Mignogna, my editor; Karin Paprocki, my art director; and Katherine Devendorf, my managing editor, who literally weathered many storms (floods, hurricanes, ice storms, and blizzards) to create this very special book. Your vision, unwavering support, and maniacal focus to detail helped to make my dream of a book from the perspective of MacKenzie Hollister a reality. YAY US!!

Daniel Lazar, my friend and INCREDIBLE agent! The Dork Diaries series has taken us on this wonderful journey together! Although it's been eleven books, this is just the first chapter of many great things to come.

A special thanks to my Team Dork staff at Aladdin/Simon & Schuster: Mara Anastas, Mary Marotta, Jon Anderson, Julie Doebler, Jennifer Romanello, Faye Bi, Carolyn Swerdloff, Lucille Rettino, Matt Pantoliano, Christina Pecorale, and the entire sales force. You're the BEST team an author could ask for!

To Torie Doherty-Munro at Writers House; my foreign rights agents Maja Nikolic, Cecilia de la Campa, and Angharad Kowal, and to Deena, Lori, Zoé, Marie, and Joy—thanks for helping me to spread the DORKINESS!

And last but not least, Erin, Nikki, Kim, Doris, and my entire family! Thank you for believing in me! I LOVE YOU ALL SO MUCH!

Always remember to let your inner DORK shine through!

The past twenty-four hours of my life have been so disgustingly NAUSEATING that I'm actually starting to feel like a . . . puddle of . . . um, cat . . . VOMIT!!

First I ruined my brand-new sweater with a PBJ and pickle sandwich (a long story).

Then I got hit in the face by a dodgeball during gym in front of the ENTIRE class and ended up trapped in a wacky fairy tale (an even longer story!).

Okay, I can handle the utter HUMILIATION of walking around school OBLIVIOUS to the fact that a SANDWICH is stuck to my abdomen like duct tape.

Hey, I can even handle a mild concussion. However, what I CAN'T handle is the fact that "someone" started an AWFUL rumor about me!

I overheard two CCP (Cute, Cool & Popular) girls gossiping about it in the bathroom.

Rumor has it that my CRUSH kissed me (at a charity event last weekend) on a DARE merely to snag a FREE large pizza from Queasy Cheesy!

Of course I totally FREAKED when I heard it! Not only is a dare like that rude and insensitive, but it's a very cruel joke to play on a person like . . . well . . . ME!

I was SURE the whole thing was a big fat LIE! Sorry! But everyone knows Queasy Cheesy pizzas are just NASTY! Had it been a dare for a yummy Crazy Burger, I'd TOTALLY believe it!

Hey, I'll be the first to admit, that rumor could have been A LOT worse. But STILL . . . !! I just wish "someone" would stay out of my personal business. And by "someone," I mean my mortal enemy . . . MACKENZIE HOLLISTER ☹!!

I don't know why that girl HATES MY GUTS! It wasn't MY fault Principal Winston gave her a three-day detention for "unsportsmanlike behavior" for slamming me in the face with that dodgeball.

I'm really LUCKY I'm not in a COMA right now!
Or undergoing life-threatening surgery . . .

Anyway, as punishment for what MacKenzie did to me, she has to clean the bug-infested showers in the girls' locker room.

Unfortunately, I learned today that the bug problem in there is REALLY bad!!

I was sitting behind MacKenzie in French class finishing up my homework when I noticed there was something stuck in her hair.

At first I thought it was one of those fancy designer barrettes she loves to wear. But when I took a closer look, I realized it was actually a gigantic dead STINK BUG!! EWW ☹!!

That's when I tapped her on the shoulder. "Um, MacKenzie! Excuse me, but I just wanted to let you know that—"

"Nikki, WHY are you even talking to me?! Just mind your OWN business!" she said, glaring at me like I was something her spoiled poodle, Fifi, had left in the grass in her backyard.

4

← BUG

MACKENZIE, GLARING AT ME
IN A VERY RUDE MANNER!

"Okay! Then I won't tell you there's a huge dead STINK BUG in your hair!" I said very calmly. "Besides, it kinda looks like an ugly barrette! And it totally complements your eye color!"

"WHAT?!" MacKenzie gasped, and her eyes got as big as saucers.

She whipped out her makeup mirror.

"OMG! OMG! There's a big black . . . INSECT with prickly legs tangled in my golden tresses! EEEEEEEEEEEK!!!" she shrieked. Then she started jumping around hysterically and shaking her hair to get it out. She had a complete meltdown!

"You're making it worse. Now it's even more tangled in there. Just sit down and chillax!" I said as I grabbed a tissue and reached for her hair.

"GET AWAY FROM ME!!" she screamed. "I don't want TWO disgusting CREATURES in my beautiful hair!"

"Stop acting like a spoiled BRAT!" I shot back.
I'm just removing the bug for you! See?!"

ME, REMOVING THE STINK BUG
FROM MACKENZIE'S HAIR

"That is DISGUSTING! Get it away from me!"

"You're welcome!" I said, glaring at her.

"Hmph! Don't expect a thank-you from me! It's all YOUR fault that bug was in my hair! It's probably from those nasty showers I'm being forced to clean."

Suddenly she folded her arms and narrowed her eyes at me.

"Or maybe YOU put it in my hair to try to ruin my reputation! I bet you want everyone to think my house is overrun with disgusting bugs! Again."

"MacKenzie, I think your lip gloss must be leaking into your brain. That's ridiculous!"

"How could you put that nasty BUG in my hair?! I'm getting SICK just thinking about it. UGH!!"

Then she covered her mouth and mumbled something. But I couldn't understand a word. . . .

8

ME, TRYING TO FIGURE OUT WHAT
MACKENZIE WAS SAYING!

Although we were in French class, it definitely
didn't sound like she was speaking French!

By the time I FINALLY figured out what she was saying, it was TOO late.

Desperate, she took off running toward the wastebasket at the front of the room.

But, unfortunately, she DIDN'T make it.

I could NOT believe that MacKenzie Hollister, the QUEEN of the CCPs, actually threw up in front of the ENTIRE French class!

She was like a bad car accident! I really DIDN'T want to see her covered in puke from head to toe ☹! But I couldn't help staring ☺!

I have never seen her SO embarrassed. SO humiliated. SO vulnerable. SO um . . . MESSY!

I was both shocked and surprised when I was suddenly overcome with overwhelming emotion.

I had NEVER, EVER felt more SORRY for a human being in my ENTIRE life! . . .

POOR CHUCK THE JANITOR!!
HE HAS A REALLY DIRTY JOB!

It seemed like such a grave injustice that HE had to clean up the horrible mess that MacKenzie had made.

Sometimes life is SO UNFAIR ☹!!

But he took his job very seriously because he actually put on one of those paper mask thingies that doctors wear during surgery.

I'm guessing it was probably because of the very noxious and excessive . . . STINKAGE!

Anyway, our French teacher immediately sent MacKenzie down to the office to call her parents to go home for the rest of the day.

And instead of having class in our smelly, contaminated room, our teacher took us down to the library to quietly study our French vocabulary words.

Which was PERFECT for me because I was able to work on my special project for National Library Week later this month.

My BFFs, Chloe and Zoey, and I held a book drive for our school back in September, and it was a HUGE success.

So now we're planning an even bigger one for National Library Week!

We'll also be traveling to NYC for a book festival and will get to "Meet-n-Greet" some of our favorite authors. SQUEEEEEEE!!!

Anyway, I can't believe MacKenzie ACTUALLY thinks I put that stink bug in her hair!!

Unfortunately for her, it looks like the kids in our class are already GOSSIPING about what happened.

One girl had her cell phone out. She showed it to a guy, and then they started snickering like crazy.

I guessed that she was probably texting the ENTIRE school!

But this whole thing is all MacKenzie's fault!!

She totally OVERREACTED and FREAKED OUT even after I offered to help her.

MacKenzie is such a VOMIT QUEEN!

OOPS! I meant . . .

DRAMA QUEEN!

Sorry about that, MacKenzie!!

☺!!

I'm SO upset right now I can barely write ☹!!
I was at my locker, minding my own business, when
MacKenzie tapped me on my shoulder and sneered,
"Why are YOU always hanging around here?!!
PLEASE! Just go away!"

"Sorry, but I hang around here because, unfortunately,
MY locker is right next to YOURS," I said, rolling my
eyes at her.

"I still can't believe you put that bug in my hair!
I'll NEVER speak to you again as long as I live!!"

"Whatever, MacKenzie!" I muttered as I counted
down in my head for her to start blabbing at me
again. Five . . . four . . . three . . . two . . .

"You're MAD at me because I spilled the beans that
Brandon kissed you on a DARE just to get a free
pizza! And now everyone is gossiping about it. So
to get even, you PRETENDED to be injured in gym
class just to get ME in trouble! . . ."

"NIKKI, YOU'RE JUST A PATHETIC FAKE!"

Sorry, but I could only take so much of Miss Thang talking TRASH right to my face like that! So I got all up in HER face and said . . .

"Really, MacKenzie?! You think I'M faking?!! Does this BRUISE look FAKE to you?! I don't think so! The ONLY fake things around here, girlfriend, are YOUR bad hair extensions and tacky spray-on tan!!"

ME, SHOWING MACKENZIE MY BRUISE

"Poor baby! So, I'm supposed to feel guilty when I actually did you a big FAVOR?" MacKenzie snarled. "That cute little bruise I gave you draws attention away from your hideous face!"

"Um, MacKenzie, have you looked at YOUR face lately? What brand of makeup did you use this morning? Paint-by-number?!"

"I wouldn't go there if I were you. My designer lipstick cost MORE than your entire ugly outfit. So don't HATE me because I'm BEAUTIFUL!"

"Well, you need to EAT some of your designer lipstick. Then MAYBE you'll be BEAUTIFUL on the INSIDE!" I shot back.

Suddenly MacKenzie got SUPERserious and stared at my forehead.

"Nikki, I'm really worried about that bruise. It looks like gangrene might be setting in. I need to run down to the nurse's office and get some bandages for you. Wait right here, okay, hon?"

But I already knew what was going on in that TWISTED little BRAIN of hers. . . .

MACKENZIE, PUTTING A
BANDAGE ON MY BRUISE!

When she got done with me, I was going to look like a . . . totally messed up . . . middle school, um . . . MUMMY!

And I was NOT about to let MacKenzie publicly HUMILIATE me! Again!

It was bad enough that she was spreading a nasty rumor about me. But now I was worried she was going to ruin my friendship with Brandon.

Anyway, I was getting my books out of my locker and still FUMING about everything she'd done to me, when I felt ANOTHER tap on my shoulder!

JUST GREAT ☹!! The last thing I wanted to deal with right then was a second round of harassment from MacKenzie. I was so NOT letting her put bandages on my bruise!

That's when I totally lost it! I wanted to shove her bandages right down her throat. But since I don't believe in violence, I decided to just tell her off in a very RUDE yet friendly way. . . .

OMG!! When I turned around and saw it was BRANDON, I totally FREAKED OUT!!

His mouth dropped open and he looked hurt and confused. I guess I was in shock or something, because when I tried to explain why I'd said those things and apologize, all that came out was . . .

UHH . . . ?!

We just stood there. Very awkwardly. Staring at each other for what seemed like FOREVER!

"Okay, Nikki. If that's what you really want," he finally said quietly. "I guess I was totally out of line last weekend when I . . . you know. Anyway, I owe you an apology. I'm very sorry."

"WHAT?! Brandon, I don't want or need your apology. What I'm trying to say is that I made a big mistake. Actually, I owe YOU an apolo—"

"Mistake?! Really?! Is that all it was to you?"

"Of course it was a mistake. I'd never do anything like that to you on purpose. It was a brief moment of stupidity and I'm sorry it happened. But it will NEVER happen again, I promise. You did NOT deserve that."

Brandon looked even more hurt than before.

It was almost like he didn't understand a word I was saying.

After another long silence, he took a deep breath and let out a sad sigh. "I really don't know what to say. . . ."

"Actually, Brandon, you don't have to say anything at all. I was really angry. And, as crazy as it sounds, I thought you were someone else."

"I know I could have been more honest with you. But I didn't mean to mislead you. Just don't be mad at me, okay?"

"You don't understand! I was actually mad at—"

"I DO understand, Nikki, and I want you to be happy. So I'll just back off, if that's what you really want."

He nervously brushed his shaggy bangs out of his eyes and glanced at his watch.

"Anyway, I think we BOTH better get to class. Later." Then he shoved his hands in his pockets and quickly walked away. . . .

24

ME, TOTALLY CONFUSED ABOUT WHAT JUST
HAPPENED BETWEEN BRANDON AND ME ☹!

MUST. NOT. PANIC!!!

Did I really just ACCIDENTALLY tell Brandon I was sick and tired of him making my life miserable and to go slither under a rock?!!

Yep! I think I actually DID!!

Okay, time to PANIC!!! . . .

AAAAAAAAAAAAAHHH ☹!!!
(That was me screaming!)

OMG! Like, WHO does that to their CRUSH?!!

I sighed, collapsed against my locker, and blinked back tears of frustration.

A massive wave of insecurity hung over me like a dark storm cloud as I carefully contemplated my next move:

1. Just "Shake It Off" and get to my geometry class since I had a quiz starting in less than two minutes (and I still needed to study) ☹!

2. Follow Brandon around the school "stalker-style" and apologize profusely until he finally accepts and agrees that we're best buds again.

3. Rush to the girls' bathroom, lock myself in a stall, and have a meltdown until Chloe and Zoey come and rescue me (AGAIN!).

4. Climb into my locker, slam the door shut, and stay in there SULKING until the last day of school or until I DIE of hunger, whichever occurs first!

I am the WORST! FRIEND!! EVER!!!

And now ~~I THINK~~ BRANDON HATES ME!!

☹!!

FRIDAY, APRIL 4

Today we only had a half day of school due to teacher training. Which means I didn't get a chance to talk to Chloe and Zoey about that big blowup I had with Brandon yesterday.

The crazy thing is that I think I'm more upset about it today than I was yesterday. Go figure!

I stopped by Brandon's locker a couple of times to try to talk to him, but he was never around.

So now I'm starting to suspect that he might be avoiding me. If I were him, I'd avoid me too!

I really want to believe MacKenzie made up that stupid rumor about the Prank-4-Pizza—but what if all (or some?) of it is actually TRUE ☹?!!

NONE of this makes sense! So in spite of all the craziness with Brandon yesterday, I'll still consider him a true friend. He deserves it.

The Brandon I know would NEVER, EVER accept a dare like that. And I REFUSE to waste any more of my time OBSESSING over it.

Anyway, after school I was doing my biology homework when my bratty little sister, Brianna, came skipping into my room, singing to herself.

"I've got a surprise! I've got a surprise!"

She poked her head over my shoulder to see what I was doing.

"Don't you wanna know what it is?" she asked.

"Nope," I answered indifferently, and continued reading.

"Well, I'm gonna show you anyway!"

That's when Brianna grinned and slammed a fishbowl on top of my biology book. Water splashed everywhere. My homework was completely soaked! . . .

BRIANNA, SPLASHING WATER ON
ME AND MY HOMEWORK!

Brianna!!" I yelled. "What are you doing?! Now my
book and homework are soaking wet! Go away!"

I took another look at the fishbowl and realized there was actually a goldfish in it.

"Where did THAT come from?"

"My teacher!" she replied. "She's letting ME babysit the class goldfish, Rover, for the entire weekend! We're gonna do lots of fun stuff together since we're best friends!"

All I could do was shake my head.

"Well, I think you need to be more careful with him. And more responsible. You could've cracked the fishbowl!"

"Responsible? What does that mean?" she asked.

"Let's see . . . how do I explain this in Nick Jr. terms?" I tapped my chin in thought. "I'll use Mom as an example. Mom feeds you, drives you to school, takes care of you when you're sick, and makes sure that you're always safe. That's called being responsible."

"Oh! NOW I understand. So, I need to be Rover's mommy!" she said eagerly.

"Yeah, something like that," I said. "Take him to your room and read him a story. I don't want any more water on my homework."

"Okeydokey!" she replied, and picked up her fishbowl. "Rover, your mommy is taking you to see her bedroom!"

I was glad she had that fish, because I figured it would keep her occupied and out of my hair.

But fifteen minutes later she came bouncing back into my room.

"Where's Rover?" I asked her.

"He's taking a bubble bath," she answered.

"WHAT?! Did you say BUBBLE BATH?!" I shrieked.

"Yep. He smelled really fishy, so I thought I'd give him a nice, warm bubble bath! That's what Mommy would do, right?"

"Brianna, are you serious?! Rover's a FISH! He's SUPPOSED to smell really fishy!"

"Well, he DOESN'T smell fishy anymore! Come take a sniff! I gotta go finish his bubble bath now. And dry him with your hair dryer. Bye!"

Oh . . . CRUD! I slammed my book shut and sighed. So much for homework!

I rushed down the hall and then peeked into the bathroom to check on poor Rover.

And, sure enough, it was just as I had feared.

He was covered in soap suds and bubbles and FLOATING in the bathroom sink!

Brianna was busy adding even more water. . . .

BRIANNA, GIVING HER
GOLDFISH A BUBBLE BATH!

"OMG! You really gave your goldfish a bubble bath? Are you crazy?!" I exclaimed. "Brianna, you cooked the darn thing!!"

"What are you talking about? Rover's really having fun. See how relaxed he is?"

Brianna stuck the dead fish right in my face. That's when I threw up in my mouth a little.

"He's FAR from relaxed!" I told Brianna. "He's not moving because he's . . . DEAD!"

"I'm his mommy, not you! And I say he's sleeping! So there!" she said, sticking her tongue out at me.

But when she asked me if Rover could borrow MY toothbrush so they could brush their teeth together at bedtime, I'd heard enough!

Obviously, something had to be done. If I let her learn the truth on her own, she'd probably need therapy for the rest of her life. Then again, Dad wasn't exactly the expert on topics like this. He'd probably just flush poor Rover down the toilet, which would be even more traumatizing to Brianna. I decided to talk to Mom about the dead fish situation tomorrow evening, as soon as she returned home from her visit with my grandma.

Sometimes having a NUTTY little sister is really challenging!! ☹!!

"Mom, do you know about Brianna's goldfish, Rover?" I asked.

"Yes, I do! And I think he'll teach her a lot about responsibility," she answered with a smile.

"Well, last night he was doing a back float in the bathroom sink," I exclaimed. "In a bubble bath!"

Mom let out a deep sigh and rubbed her temples.

"Brianna, Brianna, Brianna . . . ," she muttered in exhaustion. "What am I going to do with that child?"

"Mom, she didn't believe me when I told her Rover was dead. She loves that fish like it's her own baby! She's going to be traumatized when she finally figures out she cooked him in a bubble bath."

I remember when I had a goldfish at her age. His name was Mr. Fish-n-Chips.

All the kids in my class brought their pets to show-and-tell, so I wanted to do the same.

I put Mr. Fish-n-Chips in a box with holes in it so he could breathe, and carried him to school.

Well, you can imagine what I discovered when
I opened up that box for show-and-tell!

"I know it's going to be sad when Brianna learns
the truth. I wish there was another option,"
Mom said, shaking her head.

Suddenly her eyes lit up.

"I have an idea! And if we hurry, we can get there
before they close at nine p.m.!"

I looked at the clock and back at her in confusion.
It was 8:43 p.m.

Normally, she'd be nagging me to finish my homework
and get ready for bed.

"I don't get it! WHERE are we going?" I asked.

"Hurry!" she exclaimed as she grabbed her
coat. "I'll explain everything in the car on
the way."

MOM, ABOUT TO TAKE ME ON
A MYSTERY ROAD TRIP!

We jumped into the car and she floored it.

"Um, MOM, can you . . . SLOW DOWN?!!"

"I can't! We only have ten minutes before they close!" she yelled back.

The rest of the ride was a blur.

Before I knew it, we were parked in the middle of an empty Pets-N-Stuff parking lot. As we were getting out of the car, we saw a store clerk locking the doors.

"Oh. No. They. Didn't!" Mom yelled. "We still have a good six minutes left to shop! They can't close early!"

She jumped out of the car and stormed up to the Pets-N-Stuff door. I scurried after her.

Inside, an employee was sweeping the floor. He saw us standing there but completely ignored us. Then he rolled his eyes and turned his back to us.

"HEY!!" Mom banged her fist on the glass door. "YOU DON'T CLOSE TILL NINE! WE STILL HAVE FIVE MINUTES TO SHOP! OPEN UP!!"

ME AND MY MOM, TRYING TO BREAK
INTO A CLOSED STORE!!

The dude looked totally annoyed. He muttered some stuff that I was probably glad I couldn't hear and kept sweeping.

So Mom just kept pounding on the glass door. I was praying that it wouldn't break and shatter into a million pieces! Finally, the guy dropped the broom, unlocked the door, and poked his head out, scowling angrily.

"When the doors are locked, that's a hint for customers to get lost!" he snapped at Mom. "We're closed, lady! Deal with it!"

He was about to slam the door shut, but Mom stuck her foot in the way.

"Listen here!" she growled, waving her finger in his face. "We have a dead goldfish emergency at home, so I am NOT in a very good mood! Now, YOU'RE going to let us in so we can buy a new one, because I am NOT doing another fish funeral! Do you have any idea how traumatic a fish funeral is for a child? WELL? DO YOU?!"

"N-no, ma'am!" the guy stuttered nervously, his eyes as big as saucers.

He must've thought we had just broken out of a mental hospital or something!

"That's right! You DON'T know!" Mom continued. "So let us in! Or so help me, I'll go straight to Pets-N-Stuff national headquarters to complain about how horrific your customer service is! Do I make myself clear, young man?"

"VERY clear, ma'am!" he said, with a fake smile plastered across his face. "Please come in!"

"Hmph!" Mom stuck her nose in the air and walked into the store like she owned the place. I scrambled after her.

I have to admit, it was kind of fun watching her tell off that jerk-of-a-clerk!

We searched all the aquariums for Rover's identical twin, but no luck.

Then, just as we were about to give up, I spotted a fish the exact same size and orangey color as Rover hiding behind a small castle.

ME AND THE NEW GOLDFISH,
GETTING TO KNOW EACH OTHER!

Mom and I were so happy to have finally found our fish that we gave each other a high five.

While she was at the checkout counter paying for the brand-new Rover, I noticed a poster for a contest to win dog food near the front door.

ENTER TODAY AND WIN A
FREE ONE-YEAR SUPPLY OF

DOGGY DINER
DOG FOOD!!

NO PURCHASE NECESSARY!

Just fill out your entry form and

deposit it in the box.

Of course I immediately thought of the Fuzzy Friends Animal Rescue Center, where Brandon volunteers! A free one-year supply of dog food could really help out the center. And, who knows, I might just win!

Any money saved on food expenses would mean additional dollars that Brandon could use to care for even MORE homeless animals. That would make him SO happy! A big smile spread across my face just thinking about him.

I suddenly realized just how much our friendship meant to me. So I decided to text him a huge apology as soon as I got back to the car.

I filled out the little card with Brandon's name and address, kissed it for good luck, and then dropped it into the big box with the rest of the entries.

I was standing at the front door, waiting for my mom, when I noticed a SUPERcute guy walk out of the shop next door, listening to his tunes. Only, it wasn't just ANY SUPERcute guy. . . .

IT WAS BRANDON?!!

And he had a PIZZA!

But it wasn't just ANY pizza!

It was a QUEASY CHEESY TAKEOUT pizza ☹!!

I gasped and stared in disbelief with my face pressed against the door.

Then I screamed, "NOOOOOOO!!!"

Only, I just said it inside my head, so no one else heard it but me.

As I watched Brandon disappear around the corner, I felt like my heart had dropped into my sneakers and splattered all over the floor.

Okay, NOW I was starting to worry that the rumor WAS true!

Which also meant I had to ask myself a very difficult and potentially heartbreaking QUESTION about that KISS. . . .

Were Chloe and Zoey going to be so ANGRY at Brandon that they'd THREATEN to give him a BEATDOWN like they did at the Sweetheart Dance back in February??!!!

OMG! That fiasco was CRAY-CRAY! Especially when Chloe totally lost it and went all Karate Kid in her fancy ball gown! Of course I was also DYING to know the answers to a few other questions. Had Brandon:

1. kissed me on a DARE just to get a free pizza, as MacKenzie had alleged?

2. kissed me only because he wanted to help raise money for charity to help the needy children of the world?

Or

3. kissed me because he considered me MORE than just a good friend?

Suddenly I felt SO confused!

It was quite obvious that I didn't know Brandon as well as I thought I did.

Anyway, by the time my mom and I finally made it back home, Brianna was fast asleep.

We tiptoed into Brianna's room and made the swap.

And as we were leaving, I could see the new Rover happily swimming around in circles.

Mission. Accomplished!!

By then I was so exhausted by the whole Brandon drama that I went straight to bed.

But I just lay awake, staring at the ceiling and trying to figure out what went wrong in our relationship.

Then I got up and started writing in my diary.

Suddenly it made perfect sense why Brandon had been so defensive on Thursday and seemingly eager to back off and give me some space.

It was probably his GUILTY conscience!

Or maybe he just wanted to start hanging out with MacKenzie.

Which is perfectly fine with me! MISS DIVA and MR. DARE totally deserve each other!!

Right now I'm so OVER Brandon!

I wouldn't care if he took a bite of his stupid pizza and CHOKED on a PEPPERONI!

I just want OFF this crazy emotional roller coaster!

☹!!

Brianna snuck into my room while I was sleeping.

"BOO!" she shouted into my ear, and giggled.

"Good morning, Brianna," I answered without flinching (after the hundredth time, it doesn't even scare me anymore). "Why don't you go somewhere and pick your nose so I can sleep?"

"Rover wanted to say hi!" she said, holding the fishbowl up to my face. "He finally woke up from his nap! See?"

The new Rover was STILL happily swimming around in circles. Thank goodness!

"And he still smells nice and clean from his bath!" she chirped. "You wanna sniff?"

"No! What I WANT is for you and Rover to get out of my room. Please!" I grumped, and threw my blanket over my head.

"We're gonna play dolls and watch TV. And then I'm gonna feed Rover a yummy breakfast!"

When Brianna said "breakfast," I assumed she'd be feeding him FISH FOOD! NOT . . .

PRINCESS SUGAR PLUM CEREAL!!

OMG! I was SO disgusted with Brianna!

Mom and I could be sitting in jail for practically breaking and entering a closed pet store.

All because Brianna didn't know how to take care of her stupid fish!

But one thing was clear! We needed to get poor Rover back to school before Brianna KILLED him. AGAIN!

Mom called Brianna's teacher to apologize and let her know that we had to replace the goldfish.

But apparently, not even the Rover that Brianna had brought home was the original Rover.

Her teacher explained that, unfortunately, other children before Brianna had also had similar "accidents."

Which meant the Rover we'd just bought was actually Rover the Ninth!

I was really shocked and surprised to hear that news.

Mom and I both agreed that Brianna was nowhere near ready for a real, live pet goldfish yet.

Although, I could always buy some of those Goldfish snack crackers and dump them in the fishbowl with a little bubble bath.

As long as they floated upside down on their backs (like the original Rover), Brianna would NEVER know the difference!

Anyway, since she has to return Rover to her classroom tomorrow, she's decided she wants to buy a pet fish with arms so it can play dolls and bake chocolate cupcakes with her.

I was like, "Sorry, Brianna! But fish DON'T have arms!"

But she said, "Uh-huh, they do! I saw one on the Internet and I'm already saving my allowance!" . . .

BRIANNA'S PET FISH WITH ARMS
(ALSO KNOWN AS A MERMAID)

Well, one thing is for sure!

If Brianna gives her NEW pet fish with arms a bubble bath and feeds her Princess Sugar Plum Cereal like she did with Rover, things could get a whole lot MESSIER really fast! I'm just sayin' . . . !!

With all the Rover drama, I completely forgot to mention the MOST important thing that happened today!!

I got frantic texts from both Chloe and Zoey about a crazy rumor they'd just heard about ME that involved Brandon, a pizza, and a kiss ☹!!

Of course I told them EVERYTHING. They both rushed over to my house and we talked for what seemed like hours.

Now I'm feeling a lot better. Maybe my life isn't a bottomless pit of despair after all!

Chloe and Zoey are the BEST friends EVER!! I don't know what I'd do without them! ☹!!

It was another typical day in gym class. The exercises were pointless, the CCP kids were slacking off, and the gym teacher was yelling at them.

I was still fuming about the Brandon situation.

"I CAN'T believe it! It's like I've been bought and sold for a cruddy pizza!" I ranted.

Since it was still a bit too chilly to play tennis outside, we practiced inside by hitting tennis balls against the gym wall.

It was actually very therapeutic for me since I needed something to help burn off all the negative energy I had pent up inside.

To put it bluntly, I was so TICKED OFF, I wanted to SMACK something!

But on a more positive note, my BFFs and I looked SUPERcute in our chic tennis outfits. . . .

ME AND MY BFFS, CHATTING
AND HITTING TENNIS BALLS IN
OUR CUTE-N-CHIC OUTFITS!

"I thought Brandon was a really nice guy. But I didn't really know him at all!" I fumed.

"Nikki, just calm down!" Zoey said. "I know it looks like the rumor might be true. But maybe Brandon bought the pizza with his allowance?"

"Really? What IDIOT would spend a dime on a cruddy Queasy Cheesy pizza?" I shot back.

"A really HUNGRY idiot?" Chloe answered. "I got a great deal on a shrimp pizza there last week."

"But he said he owes me an apology, so that must mean the rumor is true! And WHY did he just walk away when I was trying to talk to him?" I asked.

"I'm pretty sure it was probably because you were screaming at him about RUINING your life," Zoey replied. "But I could be wrong."

"Maybe he walked away to go look for a rock. You DID tell him to go SLITHER back under a rock, right?" Chloe quipped.

"Okay, I'll admit it. That part was MY fault! I just wish I knew for sure if all the stuff MacKenzie said about a DARE is true!" I said, and whacked my ball even harder. "Because now I'll NEVER know if my very first kiss was just a big JOKE! And it's DRIVING. ME. CRAZY!!!"

I slammed my tennis ball in anger, and we barely managed to duck as it ricocheted off the wall and shot across the gym at what seemed like a hundred miles an hour.

Chloe raised an eyebrow at me. "CRAZY is an understatement! Nikki, you're BEATING your poor tennis ball like it owes you money!" she snarked.

"Sorry!" I muttered.

Suddenly Zoey's eyes lit up. "Listen up, guys! I have an idea! And yes, I know it's crazy! But why don't we just call Queasy Cheesy and ask them to send us a copy of Brandon's receipt?! Then we can see if he personally paid for the pizza or if someone bought it for him because of a dare like MacKenzie said."

"Sorry, Zoey, but Queasy Cheesy would NEVER send a customer receipt to a bunch of silly, nosy girls like US!" I grumbled.

"I bet they would if they thought the silly, nosy girls were CUSTOMERS!" Chloe squealed as she did jazz hands. "All we have to do is pretend to be BRANDON!"

"OMG! That would totally work," Zoey agreed excitedly. "We'll call and say he lost his receipt and needs a new copy. We can ask them to text a copy to us."

"Are you guys NUTS?!" I practically screamed at my BFFs. "We can't pretend to be Brandon! Aren't there laws against that kind of thing?!"

That's when Chloe and Zoey gave each other "the look."

ME, VERY SUSPICIOUS THAT
CHLOE AND ZOEY ARE PLOTTING
TO BAMBOOZLE ME!

And I knew from experience that "the look" meant
they were going to try to SWEET-TALK me into
doing something I DIDN'T want to do!

I absolutely HATE being BAMBOOZLED ☹!!

"Okay, Nikki. Just forget about it!" Zoey said, suddenly looking extremely bored as she bounced her tennis ball on her racket. *BOUNCE. BOUNCE. BOUNCE. BOUNCE.* "If you want to live your life and then DIE not ever knowing if your first kiss was possibly TRUE LOVE, go right ahead!"

Chloe yawned and picked at her nails. "Well, Nikki, the good news is that when you're old and lonely, you can always spend your last days pondering whether or not Brandon bought his pizza with cash or won it from a dare. Cash or dare. Cash or dare. Cash or dare. Cash or—"

"Okay, guys! STOP IT!! Just STOP!" I yelled at them.

Unfortunately, their BAMBOOZLING was working.

As usual.

"You've made your point," I continued. "This thing could haunt me for the rest of my life. I DO want to know the truth. But I DON'T want to end up in jail trying to find out. And most important, I don't want to give MacKenzie the satisfaction of RUINING my first kiss! So what I'm trying to say is that I'd really appreciate your help on this, guys."

We happily did a three-way fist bump to show our solidarity as BFFs and our commitment to uncovering the truth behind the rumor.

"Okay, my biggest worry is that Queasy Cheesy would never believe us," I explained. "WHY would Brandon suddenly need an emergency copy of an old pizza receipt from two days ago?!"

"Well, I dunno. Maybe he needs it for, um . . . tax purposes?" Zoey said.

"Tax purposes?! Hmm, that DOES sound really legit," I said, tapping my chin, deep in thought. "You know what, Zoey?! I think it just might work!"

"I agree! It's brilliant! Pure genius!" Chloe said excitedly. "Um, what does 'for tax purposes' mean?"

"Actually, I don't have the slightest idea." Zoey shrugged. "But whenever my parents lose a receipt or important papers, people always send them new copies whenever they say it's for tax purposes."

"Yeah, I've heard my parents use that excuse too," I agreed. "And it works like a charm!"

"Wow! I think I'm going to try that the next time I bomb on a test!" Chloe snickered. "I'll just tell my teacher I lost the test paper with the bad grade and request a new test for tax purposes. Getting a do-over on a test for tax purposes could really boost my grades."

"Sorry, Chloe, but I don't think it'll fix bad grades." Zoey giggled.

"Hey, it wouldn't hurt to try!" Chloe grinned.

"Anyway, I think we should make the call from the library phone so that it appears more official. Then Queasy Cheesy won't be as quick to blow us off since we're not adults," Zoey explained.

"Why don't we call during lunch tomorrow?" I suggested. "Hardly anyone hangs out in the library during lunch on Tuesdays."

Chloe insisted on being the one to make the call as Brandon. She reasoned that since she'd read the most teen novels with hunky guys in them, she could really "get inside their heads."

Whatever that means!

We also decided to have the receipt texted to Zoey's cell phone since it has better reception in the library than Chloe's and mine.

My assignment is to pick up three library shelving assistant passes from the school office so we can leave the cafeteria during lunch to hang out in the library.

And yes! I feel a little guilty about getting LSA
passes to work in the library when we don't actually
plan on shelving any books.

But making that phone call to Queasy Cheesy
and getting to the bottom of all the recent
drama is a WAY more important task as far as
I'm concerned.

Because honestly, I just don't know if I can trust
Brandon anymore.

And the fact that our friendship is ending like this
is absolute TORTURE!!

☹!!

I've been a nervous wreck all morning! Very soon I'll know if that rumor MacKenzie has been spreading about Brandon is true.

I also had this really uneasy feeling, like I was forgetting to do something SUPERimportant.

As soon as gym class was over, Chloe, Zoey, and I rushed to the cafeteria and quickly snarfed down our lunches.

We were about to dump our trays and head for the library when I FINALLY remembered what I'd forgotten!

Our LSA passes to the library!!! Oh, CRUD ☹!!

Unfortunately, we had to either cancel our secret plan or risk an after-school detention by SNEAKING to the library without any passes.

Although I had messed things up, Chloe and Zoey STILL insisted on making that phone call.

But the difficult task of sneaking out of the cafeteria suddenly became IMPOSSIBLE when . . .

PRINCIPAL WINSTON PARKED HIS BUTT RIGHT AT OUR TABLE AND THEN JUST STOOD THERE, LIKE, FOREVER ☹!!

Of course we didn't dare make any moves. We didn't want to RUIN our rep as quiet, studious, rule-abiding dorks.

I bet Winston would NEVER guess we regularly hung out in the janitor's closet, which was strictly off-limits to students.

Hey! It was our LITTLE secret ☺!

When I texted this to Chloe and Zoey, they couldn't stop giggling. Chloe texted back that our BIG secret was that we made prank calls from the library phone ☺! And Zoey texted that our HUMONGOUS secret was that we'd snuck into the boys' locker room ☺!

Lucky for us, Winston finally wandered over to the other side of the cafeteria to eyeball a table of football players who were having a contest to see who could shove the most mac and cheese up their nose.

We quickly dumped our trays and snuck out the door . . . behind a very smelly garbage can.

MY BFFS AND ME, VERY STEALTHILY
SNEAKING TO THE LIBRARY BEHIND
A VERY SMELLY GARBAGE CAN!

Since we had been delayed by Principal Winston, by the time we made it to the library we had less than three minutes to make our phone call and get to class.

We excitedly huddled around the phone as Chloe dialed the number.

"What's up, bro! Is this Queasy Cheesy? Cool! Yo, my name is Brandon and I was in there a few days ago snagging a pizza and, dude, I lost my receipt. And I, like, really need that receipt for, um . . . tax purposes. . . . Huh? I said tax purposes! . . . No, NOT tacks porpoises. Hey, bro, this has nothing to do with thumbtacks or those big fish that look like dolphins, okay? I said TAX! PURPOSES! . . . Yeah, that's it! Cool! . . . Do I remember what I ordered? Of course I do! Not all guys are stupid. We can remember lots of stuff. I ordered . . . um . . . ! Could you hold on a second? I have to . . . burp? It's a guy thing, ya know?"

Zoey and I both cringed.

74

Chloe put her hand over the receiver and whispered frantically, "Nikki, he wants to know what my order was! Do you know what Brandon ordered?"

"Actually, Chloe, I'm not sure what his order was!" I whisper-shouted. "I never saw him actually eating it. But whatever it was, it was in the pizza box he was carrying. I'm guessing it was probably a large pizza. Oh, I almost forgot, he also had a soda bottle on top of the pizza box."

Chloe continued into the phone. "Well, DUDE! It's like this. Actually, I'm not sure what I ordered since I never saw myself eating it. But whatever it was, it was in the pizza box I was carrying! I'm guessing it was probably a large pizza. And I drank a soda that was on top of my pizza box. Did you get all that, bro?"

Zoey and I both did a giant eye roll.

I was worried sick that at some point the Queasy Cheesy guy was going to assume Chloe was a prank call and just hang up on her.

Chloe went on. "So you want to know the date and time? Um, of course I know that. But hold on, I have to go spit. Most football players spit, and I play a lot of football, fo' sure! Be right back!"

It was like Chloe had lost her mind. Why was she saying all that crazy stuff?!

"Nikki, he wants the date and time!" Chloe whispered nervously.

"Um, okay. Brianna accidentally killed her fish on Friday, and we picked up a new one Saturday night. I saw Brandon from the Pets-N-Stuff door a little after nine p.m. But please! You don't have to tell him every little detail since it's none of his business."

Chloe cleared her throat. "Okay, listen up, dude. My best friend's little sister killed her fish on Friday and my friend picked up a new one Saturday night. Then I saw um . . . . myself from the Pets-N-Stuff door a little after nine p.m. But I don't have to tell you every little detail since it's none of your business. Got that, bro? Great! . . . Okay, I'll hold."

Zoey and I shook our heads in disbelief.

My fear was that Chloe had probably been placed on hold so that the manager could call the FBI to report a suspicious caller trying to gain access to private customer info to commit identity theft or something.

The call would be traced to us in the school library and a SWAT team of twenty-nine officers would come crashing through the windows to take us into custody.

Then after what seemed like forever . . .

"OMG! You actually found the receipt and are going to send it! SQUEEEE!" Chloe squealed.

Then, assuming her phony identity, she quickly added, "WHOA! I don't know what came over me. THAT was weird! Sorry, dude. What I actually meant to say was, you found my receipt and will text it to me?! That's cool, bro, very cool!"

CHLOE, ZOEY, AND ME, HAPPY AND RELIEVED
THAT QUEASY CHEESY AGREED
TO SEND THE RECEIPT!

Chloe gave the guy Zoey's phone number and then continued. "Thanks a lot, dude! I love you, bro! To infinity and beyond! Later!"

Then she hung up the phone and gushed, "We did it! He's texting the receipt to Zoey right now!"

I couldn't believe that Chloe had actually pulled it off.

She was absolutely HORRIBLE and terribly HILARIOUS, all at the same time.

We were SO happy that we did a group hug ☺!!!

I consider myself really lucky to have great BFFs like Chloe and Zoey.

We waited nervously for the text to arrive, and when it finally did, Zoey handed her cell phone to me.

My hands were practically shaking as I read over Brandon's receipt. . . .

```
~~~~~~~~~~~~~~~~~~~~~~~~~~~~~~~~~~~~~~

        QUEASY CHEESY
           TAKEOUT
   ─────────────────────────────
    THE WORLD'S BEST PIZZA
    SATURDAY, APRIL 5  9:04 P.M.
          **RECEIPT**

   1 LARGE MEAT LOVERS PIZZA     $9.99

   1 COLA DRINK                  $1.21

   TAX & DEPOSIT                 $0.80

   TOTAL                        $12.00

   CASH                          $0.00

   QC GIFT CARD                 $12.00

   CHANGE DUE                    $0.00
   ─────────────────────────────
        **THANK YOU!**

~~~~~~~~~~~~~~~~~~~~~~~~~~~~~~~~~~~~~~
```

I blinked in shock and disbelief and read the receipt over several times.

Brandon had _NOT_ purchased the pizza from Queasy Cheesy with cash ☹!!!

Which meant that MacKenzie WAS telling the truth!

It had been paid for with a gift card! A gift card that, according to MacKenzie, had been won from a DARE that involved ME!

That little receipt told me a lot more than just the type of pizza Brandon had ordered.

It revealed that . . .

The rumor was TRUE!!

MacKenzie was RIGHT!!

Brandon was NOT MY FRIEND!!

And my very first kiss was a complete and utter SHAM!!

AAAAAAAAAAHHH!!
(That was me screaming!!!)

☹!!

WEDNESDAY, APRIL 9

Today I had a meeting with Mr. Zimmerman, the adviser of our school newspaper, about the advice column I secretly write, Just Ask Miss Know-It-All.

Since my week has been a complete nightmare, I half expected him to FIRE me on the spot!

I nervously poked my head into his office. "Hi, Mr. Zimmerman, you wanted to see—"

"NO! I don't want any!" he yelled. "NOW GET OUT OF MY OFFICE!!"

"I'm SO sorry!" I gasped, and turned to leave.

"Wait a minute, Nikki! YOU can come in! But NOT those kids who smell like Doritos and video games," he muttered.

Mr. Zimmerman is actually a nice teacher! He's just VERY . . . um, WEIRD!

It took me a while to get used to his high-strung personality and the fact that he spirals through at least five different moods daily. Which means I never quite know which one I'm going to have to deal with.

I slowly peeked inside his office again to find him slumped over his desk with sunglasses on.

His office was messy, with stacks of paper piled everywhere.

He gestured for me to have a seat, so I timidly walked over and sat down.

"PLEASE! DON'T WALK SO LOUDLY!! I HAVE A SPLITTING HEADACHE!" he grumbled.

"I–I'm really sorry!" I stammered. "I didn't know!"

"Yes, you DID! I just TOLD you a few seconds ago. I said please don't walk so loudly, I have a splitting headache. Don't you remember?!"

ME, TRYING TO APOLOGIZE TO
MR. ZIMMERMAN FOR ~~TALKING~~
WALKING TOO LOUDLY!

"Um, okay then," I said, and quickly changed the subject. "Anyway, I'm here because you wanted to see me about my Miss Know-It-All column. I hope everything is okay?"

"Actually, your advice column is more popular than ever! You're on your way to becoming the next Oprah! Keep up the good work!"

Then he explained that to make it easier to answer the large volume of mail I was receiving, he had arranged for the computer club to design a Miss Know-It-All website.

So now students needing advice can either leave a handwritten letter in one of my help boxes located around the school or e-mail me!

Thanks to Mr. Zimmerman, I have my very own Miss Know-It-All website.

This is actually great news. Although, it's about time SOMETHING went right, for once in my life.

MY BRAND-NEW
MISS KNOW-IT-ALL WEBSITE ☺!

Mr. Zimmerman said that Lauren, his intern, would
also scan the handwritten letters and e-mail them
to me to be stored on the website.

This will make my job A LOT easier!

Then he reached into his pocket and handed me a
crumpled-up Post-it note.

"Now, here's the info for your site. Your user ID is on the second line, and your password is on the third line."

"This is highly sensitive information! So guard it with your life! And if you don't, you're automatically FIRED!" he said solemnly.

"FIRED?!" I gulped. "Really?!"

"Yes, really! It took me almost four hours to set up that user ID and password! And now I can't find my to-do list. It'll be easier and less time-consuming for me to just FIRE you than spend another four hours setting up new ones. So please! Don't mess this up!"

I wanted to mention that it looked to me like my user ID and password WERE his to-do list.

But since Mr. Zimmerman was already having a rough day with his headache and all, I didn't want to risk upsetting him again.

So I just smiled, thanked him, and stuck the note in my pocket.

Then, using my new user ID and password, we logged into the website and he explained how everything worked.

I can't wait to start answering letters using the new site. Working on my advice column is going to be more fun than ever!

"Is there anything else?" he finally asked, glancing at his Ninja Turtles clock on the wall.

"No, I don't think so," I answered. "But I want to thank you again for my new Miss Know-It-All site!"

"You're very welcome!" Mr. Zimmerman said, adjusting his sunglasses and slumping back down in his chair. "NOW GET OUT OF MY OFFICE!! I've wasted enough time talking to you! And I STILL have to find my missing to-do list!"

Anyway, after our meeting, I was absolutely certain about ONE thing!

The man is more NUTTY than a Reese's Peanut Butter Cup ☹!!

But you gotta love him ☺!!

Anyway, I'm really happy that my advice column is going so well, even though the rest of my life is in SHAMBLES.

OMG! I just got the most brilliant idea!

I should write a letter to Miss Know-It-All!

Then maybe I'll give MYSELF great advice on how I can solve all my OWN personal problems!

☺!!

NOTE TO SELF:

EXTREMELY IMPORTANT INFO!!

Miss Know-It-All advice column website:

User ID: 1Buymilk

Password: 2Yogaclassat7pm

Remember to guard this with your life!!

Or you're AUTOMATICALLY FIRED!!

☹!!

I arrived at school early to work on my Miss Know-It-All advice column. It was the perfect distraction from all the drama I've been dealing with lately.

I just hoped I wouldn't run into you-know-who. Since our big fight last week, he and I have basically ignored each other.

When I walked into the newspaper office, the first thing I saw was a group of kids laughing hysterically at a video they were watching on a cell phone.

Apparently, the guy showing it had gotten it from a girl who'd recorded a classmate.

Since I love funny videos as much as the next kid, I decided to stop and check it out.

OMG!! It was so SHOCKING, I almost lost the oatmeal I ate for breakfast! It was a video of . . .

MACKENZIE HOLLISTER,
HAVING A MELTDOWN ABOUT THAT
STINK BUG IN HER HAIR!!

There she was in our French class, screaming, jumping up and down, and shaking her head like she'd lost her mind.

And get this! Someone had added MUSIC to the video. So it looked like she was doing that wacky dance that was all the rage for a hot minute called the Harlem Shake!

It was really painful to watch ☹! But I did watch. Because it was HILARIOUS ☺!!

If/when MacKenzie finds out kids are passing around that AWFUL video of her, she's going to have an EPIC meltdown.

And it'll be ten times WORSE than the one she had over that stupid stink bug.

I have to admit, that video is just . . . CRUEL!!

Although MacKenzie is NOT my favorite person, I feel really, really SORRY for her ☹!

NOT ☺!!

Hey, I'm STILL traumatized from the time she took that video of me dancing and singing onstage with Brianna at Queasy Cheesy.

And then POSTED IT ON YOUTUBE ☹!!

A VERY EMBARRASSING VIDEO OF
ME DANCING AND SINGING ONSTAGE
WITH MY LITTLE SISTER!

Maybe now MacKenzie will know what it feels like to be so utterly HUMILIATED that all you want to do is dig a very deep HOLE . . .

CRAWL into it . . .

And DIE!! ☹!!

I really hope this experience teaches her a valuable lesson.

But she can consider herself LUCKY!

At least no one has put HER video on the INTERNET for millions of people to watch.

YET!!

☺!!

FRIDAY, APRIL 11

Dear Nikki,

Sorry, but I think you've just LOST something very IMPORTANT ☺!

(Well, other than your CUTE but ADORKABLE crush, Brandon! And maybe your PRIDE!!)

Hmm . . . now, WHAT could it be?!!

Your backpack? Nope!

Your geometry textbook? Nope!

Your French homework? Nope!

How about something from that super-tacky wardrobe of yours?

I WISH!! The world would be a much better place without your HIDEOUS polyester pants ☹!!

And where did you get those cheapo shoes?!
Let me guess. They were the FREE prize in
your McDonald's Happy Meal?!

Anyway, let me start by explaining exactly
how I got my hot little hands on YOUR most
cherished TREASURE.

Like always, I got up at exactly 6:15 a.m.,
showered, and did ten minutes of yoga.

Then I had a continental breakfast with
freshly squeezed orange juice, half a bagel
with goat cheese, and a green smoothie,
all served on a silver tray by my maid,
Olga, right in my bedroom.

BTW, green smoothies are vital in helping
me maintain my FLAWLESS complexion. Along
with weekly visits to the U-PAY WE-SPRAY
tanning salon.

Then I had to decide which of my FAB designer
looks I was going to ROCK in school today....

FRESH-N-FIERCE FASHIONISTA?!

BOHO BRAINS-N-BEAUTY?!

OR . . . SWEET CHIC-N-SASSY?!

Yes, I know! As always, I looked super GLAMFABULOUS in ALL my ensembles!

But after trying on all three and consulting with my personal stylist via Skype (she's currently on tour with Taylor Swift), I chose Sweet Chic-n-Sassy.

Since Daddy was in Europe (again!) and Mommy had an extra-early appointment at the spa for a facial, our driver, Nelson, dropped me off at school in our black limo.

Which, BTW, does NOT have a six-foot-long plastic ROACH thingy on top of it!!

Like SOME people I know.

Seriously! How HUMILIATING is that?!

Sorry, but if I had to ride around in a JALOPY with a giant INSECT on top of it . . .

OMG! I CAN'T EVEN . . . !!!

I'd BLINDFOLD myself, strike a FIERCE POSE, and PAY Nelson to RUN OVER me with my LIMO.

ME, BLINDFOLDED, GETTING
RUN OVER BY MY LIMO

I'd put a PAPER BAG over my head and THROW myself into the Grand Canyon!!

ME, THROWING MYSELF INTO
THE GRAND CANYON!!

Or I'd smear DOUBLE CHEESEBURGERS all over my body and then JUMP into the SHARK TANK at Sea World!!

ME, ABOUT TO JUMP INTO
THE SHARK TANK AT SEA WORLD!!

Actually, I'm just kidding, hon ☺!!

That GINORMOUS plastic roach is apparently an important member of your family. Because YOUR little sister told MY little sister that his name is MAX and he's the family PET!

Nikki, you obviously have an extremely WEIRD family!! I feel SO sorry for MAX!

Anyway, as I was saying, after Nelson dropped me off at school I headed straight to my locker to put on more lip gloss and—

OOPSIE! Someone is coming down the hall!

So, unfortunately, I have to stop writing now.

And, Nikki, you'd NEVER guess who that "someone" is!!

It's YOU, hon ☺! You and your silly friends, Chloe and Zoey, are giggling and scampering

down the hall like a pack of socially
challenged CHIPMUNKS!

You obviously have no idea that your precious
little DIARY is missing!! Yes! I said DIARY!!

I can't wait to see you have a BIG FAT HISSY FIT
when you finally realize it's gone!

But for now I'll just hide it in my new
Verna Bradshaw designer handbag that I
bought (on sale for 20% off!) at the mall
yesterday.

Next period I plan to get a bathroom pass
from our French teacher. And while you're
busily conjugating verbs, I'll be READING
your diary ☺!

TOODLES!

Dear Nikki,

I have no idea why you spend hours and hours writing in this stupid little diary of yours.

But let me guess! It's because you seriously need to GET A LIFE!

When I want to share my life experiences or vent about something, I just talk to Mommy and Daddy.

Of course, sometimes Mommy is super busy being a socialite and doing charity work.

And sometimes Daddy is super busy building his multimillion-dollar business empire.

But when my very dedicated parents can't spend quality time with me (which I have to admit happens far too frequently these days), I can always rely on Dr. Hadley, my therapist.

He will listen to me patiently for an
ENTIRE hour as long as Daddy pays him $480
a session. AND I get to go TWICE a week if
I want to!! How COOL is that?! I'm a VERY
lucky girl ☺! But please don't be jealous
of me, okay?

I feel really SORRY for you, Nikki, because
ALL you have for emotional support are
your very WEIRD parents. And this STUPID
little diary.

And nobody else cares about you! Except
maybe your bratty little sister, Brianna. Oh,
and Chloe and Zoey. And probably Marcy,
Violet, and Jenny. Of course, there's also
Theo and Marcus.

But Brandon? Rumor has it that he's so
OVER you ☺! Sorry, hon, but your BOO has
moved on.

My point is that YOU have no REAL friends
WHATSOEVER!

And you're insanely JEALOUS that the CCPs practically WORSHIP the ground I walk on!!

Anyway, I need to make one thing perfectly clear:

I DID NOT STEAL YOUR DIARY!

I have way too much integrity to stoop that low. Besides, Daddy would buy me an entire DIARY FACTORY in some poor third-world country if I really wanted one! Just sayin'.

He mostly gives me everything I want, especially if I throw a temper tantrum about it. And Mommy says I'm an even bigger DRAMA QUEEN than SHE is ☺! They both SO adore me!

So, yesterday I was on my way to my locker to freshen up my lip gloss. My stylist says you can NEVER wear too much lip gloss!

YOU had just rushed off to class, when I witnessed a very CATASTROPHIC event. . . .

109

ME, IN TOTAL SHOCK THAT YOUR
LOCKER DOOR DIDN'T CLOSE DUE TO
YOUR VERY UGLY PUKE-COLORED COAT!!

That coat of yours was so HIDEOUS that it gave me hives. I seriously contemplated dialing 911 for an ambulance.

But not for ME! I wanted them to transport your puke-colored coat to the city DUMP. And then BURN it as a public health hazard.

And YES, Nikki, I sincerely did try to alert you to the fact that your coat sleeve was stuck in your locker door.

But due to my severe allergic reaction to your coat, all I could muster was a weak and very hoarse whisper that you apparently didn't hear.

Of course, ALL of this was totally YOUR fault! WHY any rational HUMAN BEING would wear a PUKE-COLORED coat to school is beyond explanation, logic, and reason!!

Seriously, I CAN'T EVEN . . . !!!

Anyway, by the time I started to recover from the HORROR I'd just experienced, you had already hopped happily down the hall like some CLUELESS little bunny and disappeared.

That's when I became so worried about your open locker that I went into a full-blown PANIC ATTACK!!

What if someone stole your textbooks? Our school would suffer a financial loss!

What if someone stole your house keys? Your family's safety would be at risk!

What if someone stole your coat? They'd leave it in the woods so that a pregnant stray cat could have her kittens on it!

So, Nikki, in spite of the fact that I basically HATE YOUR GUTS (just kidding, hon ☺!), I decided to do the responsible thing and take measures to protect your most valuable and treasured personal possession.

ME, HEROICALLY CONFISCATING YOUR
DIARY BEFORE IT COULD GET STOLEN
AND READ BY THE ENTIRE SCHOOL!!

As you can see, I did not STEAL your diary!!
Actually, you should THANK ME for what
I did! Because otherwise, the pages containing
your deepest, darkest secrets would be
plastered all over the hallways by now.

I had every intention of returning your diary
to you before social studies. But I barely
got to class on time since I had to stop
by the girls' bathroom to brush my hair.

And then I planned to give it back to you
after gym class. But our gym teacher made
me run three extra laps for talking to
Jessica about your disgusting puke-colored
coat during exercises.

And lastly, I was going to give it to you
in bio. But I was preoccupied FLIRTING with
BRANDON, while you watched and pretended
that you WEREN'T insanely jealous ☺!

So at the end of the day I was FORCED to
take your diary home with me for safekeeping!

To be very honest, Nikki, I've never liked you because I didn't really know you! And I'm guessing that you probably don't like me because you don't really know me.

So the fact that I'm reading your diary is actually a GOOD thing! I'm learning about your hopes, dreams, and fears, and all your deepest, darkest secrets.

And so that YOU can get to know ME better, I'm going to write some entries in your diary about me and my life!

I'll also DRAW in your diary so that you can see what a fabulously talented artist I am.

But please! Don't believe for one minute that you are actually as pretty as I am sketching you on these pages. I refuse to draw ugly people because they literally make me nauseous!

Anyway, Nikki, I really hope you enjoy reading . . .

THE MACKENZIE DIARIES:
TALES FROM A NOT-SO-DORKY DRAMA QUEEN

WELCOME TO MY WORLD, HON!!!

TOODLES!

SUNDAY, APRIL 13

Dear Nikki,

Today was so . . . totally FREAKY! Why?

Because I had a full-blown FASHION EMERGENCY!

OMG! I got a little dizzy and my palms actually started to sweat. EWW!!

My fashion stylist (who, BTW, is now on tour with Ariana Grande) says one should NEVER sweat! One should just . . . GLOW!

Anyway, it was vital that I rush out to the mall to find the PERFECT blouse to wear to school on Monday.

It needed to be:

Cute, but not too immature.

Classy, but not too boring.

Bold, but not too tacky.

Trendy, but not too faddish.

Finally, after shopping for what seemed like FOREVER, I found not one, not two, but THREE fabulous designer blouses!

And since I couldn't make up my mind which one I loved best, I decided to buy all THREE of them for only $689.32!

WHY?! Because I COULD!!

Yay ME ☺!!

Please don't HATE me because I'm rich!!

Then I rushed home and locked myself in my bedroom.

I had to make the very difficult decision of which blouse would best complement ~~your~~ MY diary!!

ME, TRYING TO DECIDE WHICH
FABULOUS BLOUSE BEST MATCHES
~~YOUR~~ MY DIARY!

However, the last thing I needed was for
some CRAZY girl at school to SEE me with

HER DIARY and accuse me of STEALING it!

Of course, initially no one would believe her because of my reputation for being a very kind and honest individual.

But if she told Principal Winston, there was a chance I could get BUSTED with it in my purse.

Which would mean an automatic suspension from WCD!!

And what if I was forced to attend a PUBLIC school?! Just like the ones I see on television?!

EWW ☹!!

Was this diary worth ALL that?!

I took a long, hard look at myself in the mirror and decided right then and there to do the ONLY thing that made sense.

ME, VERY INGENIOUSLY COVERING
THE DIARY WITH FABRIC SO NO
ONE WILL RECOGNIZE IT!!

YES! I know! I'm a BEAUTIFUL GENIUS ☺!!

It took me TWO whole hours to cover the diary with the leopard-print fabric from my brand-new designer blouse.

And when I finally finished, I was totally blown away by how FANTASTIC it looked.

The entire experience was so exciting and inspiring that I actually started to ~~sweat~~ GLOW!

That's when I rushed right back to the mall (thank goodness it hadn't closed yet!) and purchased another designer blouse, black leather pants, boots, and sunglasses.

Because tomorrow I plan to show off ~~your~~ MY new diary to EVERYONE at school!

YAY ME!! ☺!

Anyway, even though your diary only covered nine days in April, one thing is abundantly clear, Nikki. . . .

YOU ARE
ONE. SICK. LITTLE. COOKIE!!

Seriously, I can't believe I wasted hours of my life reading all this whiny, fabricated garbage.

Everything you wrote was like, "Mackenzie did THIS to me!" and "Mackenzie did THAT to me!" as if I'M the dysfunctional one!

Are you for real?! #Girlbye!

You are DELUSIONAL if you think you're the victim here!

Just face the truth!

You've been INSANELY JEALOUS of me from day one and are OBSESSED with trying to RUIN my life!

Brandon and I would be an item by now if you hadn't made him feel SORRY for you with all your "CUTE-N-DORKY" little antics.

You are BEYOND evil, Nikki Maxwell!

And you LIE so much, you should seriously consider a career in politics!

I think YOU need my therapist, Dr. Hadley, WAY more than I do!

I realize all the stuff I'm saying to you may sound cold, cruel, and mean. But I'm just being totally HONEST with you, Nikki.

Sorry I'm NOT sorry ☺!!

TOODLES!

MacKenzie

MONDAY, APRIL 14

Dear Nikki,

Today was a super EXCITING day for me!

How was YOUR day, hon?

NOT very good? I thought so!

Especially after I saw you MOPING around
school like a sad little puppy with your
pathetic BFFs, Chloe and Zoey, trailing
behind you. You guys looked really worried
and appeared to be searching for something.

I wonder what?!

But enough about YOU! Let's talk about ME ☺!!

Didn't you just LOVE the brand-new designer
outfit that I wore to school today?

It actually matched ~~your~~ MY diary!!

ME, KILLIN' IT IN MY NEW OUTFIT
WITH MATCHING DIARY!!

I think my new leopard-print cover looks ten times better than YOUR tacky blue-jean cover.

And that cute little pocket was SO immature!

Anyway, Nikki, when you and your BFFs walked up to your locker, I was standing just inches away from you, writing in ~~your~~ MY diary!

OMG! It was SURREAL!

But because I am a very compassionate person and you were obviously super upset about something, I asked you if anything was wrong.

"Excuse me, Nikki, but WHY are you throwing your JUNK all over the hallway? This is NOT your bedroom! WHAT is WRONG with you?!" I asked sweetly.

"Sorry, Mackenzie. We'll clean up my stuff in a minute," you said, rolling your sad eyes at me. "But right now we're busy looking for something really important, okay?"

ME, WATCHING YOU DESPERATELY
SEARCH FOR YOUR LOST DIARY!!

"Oh, really? Maybe I can help you find it. So, what did you lose, Nikki?" I asked, trying my best to be helpful.

That's when you, Chloe, and Zoey nervously glanced at each other and started whispering.

"So now it's a big secret?!" I asked, getting a little impatient. "Well . . . WHAT did you lose?!"

Then the three of you answered at exactly the same time. . . .

"Homework!" said Zoey.

"Sweater!" said Chloe.

"Cell phone!" you said.

"Wait a minute!" I exclaimed, totally confused. "WHAT exactly did you lose?!"

"Sweater!" said Zoey.

"Cell phone!" said Chloe.

"Homework!" you said.

You guys were obviously LYING to me, but I just played along with your little charade.

"So you lost homework, a sweater, AND a cell phone?!" I asked suspiciously.

Chloe and Zoey answered "No!" at the exact same time that you answered "Yes!"

Then Chloe and Zoey changed THEIR answer to "Yes!" at the same exact time that you changed YOUR answer to "No!"

And get this! THEN you all gave each other dirty looks and started whispering again. But I just played right along.

"Listen, you idiots!" I said impatiently. "I was going to offer to help you FIND whatever it is that you lost! But since you obviously don't know WHAT you're looking for, I won't bother!"

"MacKenzie, thanks. But please, just mind your OWN business!" Chloe said all snotty-like.

"Yeah, we GOT this!" Zoey added, glaring at me.

Sorry, but I couldn't resist it any longer.

"Fine! Then I WILL just mind my OWN business! I just hope you didn't lose your stupid little diary, Nikki! Because if it ever gets into the wrong hands, all your DIRTY little secrets will get out and this entire school will know what a big PHONY you are! Especially Brandon!"

OMG, Nikki! When I said the "D" word—DIARY— you looked like you'd just seen a ghost!! I really wish you could have seen your face! It was PRICELESS!!

The three of you just stared at me in complete shock with your mouths dangling open.

I wanted to pull out my cell phone and take a snapshot of you guys.

And then post it at:
#YouHaveNoIdeaHowStupidYouLookRightNow.

Anyway, you and your BFFs completely TRASHED your locker!

But you STILL didn't find your diary, did you?!

POOR BABY ☺!!

Well, I better get to class!

I completely lost track of time, and the bell just rang.

I have to admit, this diary stuff is starting to get kind of addicting!

TOODLES!

MacKenzie ♡

Dear Nikki,

I'm having a HORRIBLE day today!! And it's all YOUR fault ☹!!

Today at lunch I was completely torn between the tofu salad and the tofu burger since I am very particular about what I eat.

I finally decided on the teriyaki tofu salad with honey ginger dressing and a chilled bottle of Mountain's Peak spring water. WHY? Because the tofu burger had a huge fly buzzing around it. EWW ☹!

Anyway, just as I was about to sit down at the CCP table, I saw all my friends laughing hysterically at a video of some stupid girl freaking out because she had a bug in her hair.

I was going to watch it and laugh too. Until I realized SHE was ME!!

ME, IN SHOCK THAT MY FRIENDS
ARE LAUGHING AT ME!!

Suddenly my stomach started to feel very sick and QUEASY. Not from the video, but from the flashback to that fly buzzing around the tofu burger I almost ate! YUCK 🙁!

I could NOT believe my friends would actually stab me in the back like this. Even my so-called BFF, Jessica.

I have never been so utterly HUMILIATED in my ENTIRE LIFE!! My reputation at this school is RUINED!!

I'm so upset right now I could just . . .

SCREEEEEEEEAM!! !

So, Nikki, would you like to know why I HATE you so much?!

NO, you DON'T want to know?! Well, Miss Smarty-Pants, I'm going to tell you ANYWAY!! So just deal with it! Here's my list! The SHORT one!!

10 REASONS WHY I HATE YOU!!

1. You CHEATED to WIN the avant-garde art competition!!

2. You totally RUINED my birthday party by SABOTAGING the chocolate fountain!!

3. You competed in the TALENT SHOW and landed a RECORD DEAL even though your application was INCOMPLETE (like, WHO names their band Actually, I'm Not Really Sure Yet?)!!

4. You WON the "Holiday on Ice" show, and EVERYBODY knows that you CAN'T ice-skate!

5. You TOILET-PAPERED my house!!!!

6. You tricked me into DIGGING through a DUMPSTER filled with GARBAGE in my designer dress at the Sweetheart Dance!

7. You actually KISSED my FBF (future boyfriend), BRANDON!!

139

8. You pretended to be seriously HURT during dodgeball so that I would get DETENTION (which, BTW, could totally RUIN my chances of getting into an Ivy League university)!

9. You put a nasty STINK BUG in my hair!!

And the HORRIBLE THING that I just found out TODAY . . .

10. You've completely RUINED my reputation and HUMILIATED me, because now the ENTIRE school is passing around that AWFUL video of me having a meltdown about the bug that YOU put in my hair.

I am so NOT making this stuff up!!

It's quite obvious you're trying to completely DESTROY my life!!

Things are SO bad at this school that ONE of us has to GO!

It's either YOU . . .

Or . . . ME!!

And if Principal Winston won't KICK you out of this school for RUINING MY LIFE . . .

I'M TRANSFERRING TO ANOTHER SCHOOL!!

And I mean it!! I've had it up to HERE with you, Nikki Maxwell. You are NOT going to get away with this.

Just admit it!

If YOU were ME, you'd HATE yourself TOO ☹!

TOODLES!!

MacKenzie ♡

Dear Nikki,

I'm so upset right now I could just . . .

SCREEEEEEEEAM!! !

The ENTIRE school has seen that video! And now everyone is laughing at me behind my back.

The CCP girls are giggling.

The CCP guys are chuckling.

The cheerleaders are snickering.

The football team is snorting.

The cooks in the cafeteria are cackling.

I hate to admit it, Nikki! But right now I'm an even bigger JOKE at this school than YOU are!

I was really shocked to see you and your BFFs in school today. I thought you guys were supposed to be in New York City, hanging out with your favorite authors in celebration of National Library Week!

According to the latest gossip, at the very last minute you and your BFFs decided to give your trip to Marcy, Violet, and Jenny so you guys could stay in town and work on the big book drive for the school library.

Sorry! But I don't believe that LAME excuse for one minute!

The TRUTH is, instead of enjoying the exciting sights and sounds of the most FAB city on this earth, YOU chose to stay at school moping around hopelessly depressed, digging through trash cans, scouring bathroom stalls, and searching every nook and cranny in a desperate attempt to find that precious little DIARY of yours!

OMG! I felt SO sorry for you I ALMOST shed a tear. Until I remembered my mascara might run, and goopy black tears streaming down my normally flawless face wouldn't look very CUTE.

Unfortunately, Nikki, you're NOT going to find your diary anytime soon. WHY? Because I'm sitting right next to you in class WRITING in it!

Like, how IRONIC is that ☺?!

And since you're partially responsible for me having such a ROTTEN and MISERABLE day, I thought it was only fair that I do something special for YOU so you can feel the same way.

That's why I tapped you on your shoulder and whispered, "Nikki, I just saw a book that looked exactly like your diary in the library! I think it was on a bookshelf. Or near a pile of books!"

YOU AND YOUR BFFS, SEARCHING FOR YOUR DIARY IN THE LIBRARY!

YOU AND YOUR BFFS, STILL
SEARCHING FOR YOUR DIARY
SIX HOURS LATER ☺!!

And yes, I realize that tricking you into spending countless hours searching in vain for your diary in the library was a cold and heartless prank.

But do I need to remind YOU of all the SHADY things you've done to humiliate ME?!!

For starters, you CHEATED to win the avant-garde art competition. You're definitely an artist—a CON artist ☹!

That sorry display of the tattoos that you drew was hardly what I'D call art.

Everyone knows I should have won first place!

My brilliant entry could have changed the fashion world as we know it.

My cutting-edge concept would have allowed YOU and other fashion-challenged SLOBS to undergo INSTANTANEOUS MAKEOVERS!!

MY FAB-4-EVER
INSTANT FASHION MAKEOVER KITS

My fashions are PERFECT for the cute and trendy girl who was viciously PRANKED into digging through a FILTHY Dumpster for a nonexistent piece of designer jewelry during the Sweetheart Dance!

A girl like ME ☹!!!

And if she's smelling like three-week-old Dumpster juice and has a slimy, rotten banana peel stuck to her face, both SHE and her fab fashion can easily be splashed with laundry detergent and sprayed down with a water hose right in her own backyard!

I could have made MILLIONS on this idea and become one of the hottest fashion designers in the world! But I didn't! And it's all YOUR fault, Nikki ☹!!

Anyway, I've noticed that you and Brandon barely speak to each other now that you've become totally obsessed with finding your lost diary.

It must be heart-wrenching to see your wonderful friendship with him just shrivel up and DIE like a slimy snail on a hot sidewalk.

It's no wonder you look so sad and depressed.

Mere words cannot express the intense emotions I'm feeling right now.

Except maybe . . . YAY ME ☺!!

Sorry I'm NOT sorry!

But please don't get too frustrated about not finding your diary. I have lots of great ideas for where you can look for it.

TOODLES!

Dear Nikki,

Great news!

I've finally found the PERFECT school!

All I have to do now is convince my parents to let me transfer!!

I can't believe this could actually be my very last week at this CRUDDY school!

YAY ME ☺!!

North Hampton Hills International Academy is one of the most prestigious private schools in the nation!

And it's only twenty-seven minutes from my house. Or ten minutes, if Daddy lets me fly by private helicopter.

Instead of sweaty, smelly sports like football and basketball, it has VERY classy ones, like sailing, horseback riding, fencing, and polo.

And most of the students travel abroad every year. Please don't be jealous, but I'll probably be spending the summer in PARIS ☺!

YAY ME ☺!!

And since I'm going to have lots of cool new friends, I can't wait to throw a big birthday bash at the country club and invite them all.

Thank goodness YOU won't be around to SABOTAGE my party like last time!!

I was the first person EVER at school to invite a SEWER MUTANT like you to a party!

And how did you repay my generosity ☹?!!

I can almost forgive you for scarfing down all the hors d'oeuvres like a starving barnyard animal.

I know you love wing-dings because they fill that empty void in your miserable little life.

But the coup de grâce was that stunt you pulled with the chocolate fountain.

I know there was a nasty rumor going around at school that my ex-BFF, Jessica, purposely knocked your plate of fruit into the chocolate fountain and splashed chocolate all over your new party dress just to be MEAN!

But that is so NOT true!

Jessica went so far as to PINKIE SWEAR that she saw YOUR dress get splattered while YOU were secretly dumping TRASH into the fountain to sabotage it so it would malfunction!!

YOU, AT MY PARTY, PUTTING TRASH
IN THE CHOCOLATE FOUNTAIN!!

WHY? Because you were insanely jealous that
I looked way cuter in my Dior dress than you
did in that recycled DISHRAG you were wearing.

But, Nikki, HOW could you be so CRUEL as to DRENCH me with chocolate at the moment I was taking my picture for the SOCIETY PAGE?!

ME, FREAKING OUT BECAUSE YOU RUINED MY BIRTHDAY PARTY!!

I had so much chocolate on me that I felt like a Godiva truffle with LEGS!

Then everyone started LAUGHING at me and taking PICS with their cell phones!

It was HORRIBLE!! For once I was ALMOST as UNPOPULAR as YOU!

I was so FURIOUS, I wanted to . . .

SCREEEEEEEEAM!!! 😠!!

You were lucky you left my party when you did!! Otherwise, you would've experienced what "death by chocolate" really means ☹!

Now, can I ask you a personal question about something you wrote in your diary?

WHY on earth would you write your USERNAME and PASSWORD in your DIARY?! Do you realize that some very emotionally disturbed individual could steal your diary, read it, and see this highly confidential information just sitting right there on the page?

And if the person is really CRAY-CRAY, she could break into the Miss Know-It-All advice column that you SECRETLY write for the school newspaper (according to your diary)! She could wreak TOTAL HAVOC on the entire student body! With just a few clicks, the entire world as you know it could be completely destroyed!!

Then YOU'D get blamed for cyberbullying, kicked out of school, and—

WAIT!!! ONE!!! MINUTE!!! NO! This CAN'T BE TRUE!!!!!!!

 the real MISS KNOW-IT-ALL??!!

And THIS is your real PASSWORD???!!!

OMG!! I CAN'T EVEN . . . !!

ME, ON MISS KNOW-IT-ALL,
SECRETLY VOLUNTEERING TO
HELP WITH YOUR ADVICE COLUMN!!

Anyway, you should be thankful I WARNED
you that some PSYCHOPATH could steal your

username and password, break into your
Miss Know-It-All website, and WREAK HAVOC
on the entire student body.

You're very LUCKY that I, MACKENZIE HOLLISTER,
stumbled across your information.

And NOT some deranged, vindictive, diary-snatching
DRAMA QUEEN!!

TOODLES!

Mackenzie ♡

FRIDAY, APRIL 18

Dear Nikki,

YAWN!

I'm really tired today!

Wanna know why, hon?!

Because I stayed up half the night answering letters from the LOSERS who write to your Miss Know-It-All advice column.

I must admit, I was a bit surprised by what I read. I had no idea that the students at this school led such PATHETIC lives!

Anyway, I'm super excited because on Monday, April 28, I have a big SURPRISE for you ☺!!

And when Principal Winston reads the Miss Know-It-All column that I secretly helped you write, he's going to be FURIOUS!!

You're going to get SUSPENDED for CYBERBULLYING so fast it will make your head spin!

Anyway, here are copies of my two favorite letters and the advice I gave:

* * * * * * * * * * * * * *

Dear Miss Know-It-All,

I worked really hard to make the eighth-grade cheerleading team this year, but the other cheerleaders treat me like I don't belong. I never get to do much cheering or dancing like they do.

The only time the team captain needs me is when we do the human pyramid, and she always puts me at the bottom! I have to hold the most people on my back, which is totally excruciating, and if I lose my balance, the whole pyramid collapses and everyone bullies me about it!

I'm tired of those girls walking all over me. Literally! I don't know what I did to deserve this kind of treatment, but it's pretty obvious they all hate my guts. ☹!

I'm majorly frustrated! I don't know if I should quit the team, confront my teammates, or just keep quiet so I don't make things worse. I really don't want to give up my dream of making varsity! What would you do??

—*Cheerless Cheerleader*

* * * * * * * * * * * * *

Dear Cheerless Cheerleader,

Hon . . . I think you're kidding yourself if you think you made the cheerleading team based on your awesome moves. My reliable source on the team told me your tryout routine was HOR-REN-DOUS. She said she couldn't tell if you were trying to dance or going into convulsions!

Your backflips were BACKFLOPS, your cartwheels were FLAT TIRES, and your dismount was totally DISGUSTING! Get the picture?

You were chosen for one reason, and one reason alone—you look like a sturdy ogre who can carry a lot of weight! It's been a long tradition for cheerleading captains to hand-pick strong, ugly girls for the bottom of the pyramid. Didn't you know that??

Quit taking everything so personally! Just accept that the bottom is where you belong, sweetie! You should hold your green, Shrek-looking head high that someone actually wants you for something. Bet that doesn't happen often! Yay you!

Sincerely,
Miss Know-It-All

P.S. My source wants you to stop dancing. She says you're giving the squad NIGHT TERRORS!

* * * * * * * * * * * * * * *

OMG! My letter was so MEAN!! OUCH!! 😊!!

Now, this next letter really tugged at my heartstrings. It was hard to be cruel to this poor guy, because he seemed genuinely distraught.

I felt so sorry for him that I actually e-mailed my advice response to him last night.

* * * * * * * * * * * * * *

Dear Miss Know-It-All,

I have a good friend, and she's smart, funny, and kind.

But lately we haven't been getting along and it's all MY fault. Between a nasty rumor at school and me not telling her much about my personal life, she doesn't trust me. And I don't blame her one bit.

Whenever I try to talk to her in class, she just seems down and kind of distracted, like something is really bothering her. I'm starting to worry about her, and I really miss our friendship.

What can I do to fix things?

—*Massively Cruddy Friend*

* * * * * * * * * * * * * *

Dear Massively Cruddy Friend,

It sounds like you really messed up big-time, bro!

By the way she's acting, it might be too late to rescue this relationship. It looks to me like she wants you about as much as she wants a week-old bowl of moldy oatmeal.

You need to let her know that you care about her ASAP! But NOT with a quick and impersonal e-mail or text.

Since she obviously doesn't feel comfortable talking to you, don't push her. I suggest you write a sincere apology letter and tape it to her locker right before class so that you can see her reaction. Also, make sure you ask her to meet you after school someplace classy so you can talk. Hint: Most girls LOVE the CupCakery!

If she shows up, she truly cares about you and you can consider yourself lucky that you have a very special friendship! Awwww 😊!!!

However, if your friend doesn't show up, it means she's still pretty ticked off at you and possibly never really cared to begin with. If that happens, my advice is to just get over her and move on!

Because, dude, there are plenty of fish in the sea! Including ME 😊!

Sincerely,
Miss Know-It-All

* * * * * * * * * * * * * * *

OMG!! Nikki, are YOU thinking what I'M thinking?!

It's very possible that this letter came from YOUR crush, Brandon! YAY YOU ☺!!

And if it did, I'll admit that I'm a little jealous that Brandon wrote to Miss Know-It-All about YOU and not ME!

Unfortunately, he seems to genuinely care about you in spite of the fact that you're a total LOSER!

But sometimes life is NOT fair and people get things that they DON'T deserve!

Most students work really hard to be successful.

And some are naturally gifted, like . . . ME!

Then there are people who CHEAT their way to the top, like . . . YOU!

Yes! I'm STILL traumatized by that talent show!

My dance troupe, Mac's Maniacs, WON because of my mad skillz, edgy styling, and phenomenal choreography!

We KILLED IT!!

Your DORKY band, Actually, I'm Not Really Sure Yet, was a big fat JOKE!

Seriously, Nikki, your singing sounded like a screeching cat with a violent case of diarrhea!

But in spite of the fact that I kicked your butt onstage, it was YOU who became a local celebrity, teen pop princess, and star of your very OWN reality television show!

EXCUSE ME?!! How did THAT happen?!!

You're definitely NOT pretty enough to get by on just your looks like most of the tone-deaf female pop stars today.

But I know your little secret!

You're a MASTER MANIPULATOR!

You BRAINWASH people to make them give you whatever you want!

Or you make them feel so SORRY for you that they're overcome with GUILT and give you whatever you want.

So just enjoy your fifteen minutes of fame while you can, you CHEATING, NO-TALENT POSEUR!

One thing is for sure . . . you will NEVER get invited to attend the GRAMMY AWARDS!

Unless it's to EXTERMINATE the FLIES, FLEAS, and HEAD LICE on those passed-out ROCK STARS who haven't bathed in two years!!

YOU, EXTERMINATING ROCK STARS AT THE GRAMMYS!

Just thinking about all of this makes me so mad I could just . . .

SCREEEEEEEEAM! 😠!!

But I'm not going to get MAD!!

I'm going to get EVEN! 😊!!

By helping YOU with your Miss Know-It-All column!

And to show you what a great job I'm doing, every day I'll share a few of my favorite SUPER-MEAN letters.

TOODLES!

SATURDAY, APRIL 19

Dear Nikki,

OMG! Yesterday I thought I was going to EXPLODE with excitement! You will NEVER believe what actually happened!

No, I didn't go to the mall and buy you a new wardrobe to replace the tacky clothing you purchased on clearance at Rite-Aim.

Don't LIE to me, Nikki!!

I swear! I saw YOUR JEANS right next to the adult diapers display when I stopped by there to pick up more lip gloss!

Okay, so remember that advice letter I wrote and sent to MASSIVELY CRUDDY FRIEND?

Well, Nikki, guess what I saw taped to your locker right before biology class?! And guess WHO it was from?!

172

ME, GUSHING OVER THE LETTER
BRANDON LEFT FOR YOU!!

Okay, I'll admit that it makes me ~~a little~~ ~~irritated~~ REALLY FURIOUS that Brandon seems to adore you so much.

But can you blame me?!

He's supposed to be MY boyfriend!!

And yes! I was totally DEVASTATED when I saw Brandon kiss you at that charity event!

But then I had an epiphany and totally understood why he did it.

Brandon is a kind, caring, and compassionate person.

Which is probably why he totally IGNORES ME and instead hangs out with all of those pesky, flea-infested little furballs at Fuzzy Friends every day after school!

He's also very cool, super cute, and extremely mature for his age.

Like, how many guys would literally FORCE themselves to kiss a DONKEY FACE like yours in order to save the needy children of the world?!

BRANDON, KISSING YOUR DONKEY FACE JUST TO SAVE THE NEEDY CHILDREN OF THE WORLD!!!

Then I ~~started~~ HEARD the nasty rumor that Brandon kissed you on a DARE just to get a Queasy Cheesy pizza!

So, Nikki, I hope you understand that his kiss actually meant nothing at all. Brandon and I were made for each other! He just doesn't know it yet.

And even though you don't deserve it, I DO plan to invite you to OUR wedding when we get married in ten years!

Brandon and I would be VERY honored if you'd agree to be a special guest and participate in our ceremony.

OMG! It's going to be SO romantic when we release a hundred doves as a symbol of our love soaring to new heights in the infinite sky!

And, Nikki, we'll need YOU up front with us on our special day . . .

. . . TO CLEAN UP ALL OF THAT
NASTY BIRD POOP!!

Yes, Nikki! On my wedding day I will FINALLY get even with you for making me scrub those filthy showers in detention! They were the LONGEST three days of my entire LIFE!

SERIOUSLY! That place was an ICKY mildew-and-bug-infested NIGHTMARE! There were more species of INSECTS in there than in the Amazon rain forest!!

I pulled enough HAIR out of the drains to start my own weave business! And I almost puked when I found a hairball the size of a chubby rat!

Sorry to break the news to you, Nikki, but Mackenzie Hollister DOES NOT CLEAN!

Please don't be jealous, but I've had a MAID cleaning up after me since I was three months old.

I thought all I had to do was spray stuff with that foamy cleaner and then all of those smiling Scrubbing Bubbles thingies from the commercial would show up and do all the nasty grunt work!!

But that DIDN'T happen!! I was SO confused!!

So of course I spent, like, two hours CRYING into my MOP BUCKET before my EVIL gym teacher came in and YELLED at me!!

And when I explained that the Scrubbing Bubbles thingies never showed up to help me clean, she said I was "talking crazy" and sent me down to the nurse's office for possible overexposure to toxic fumes!!

Even now, I can STILL smell the faint stench of ammonia, mildew, and "lemony-fresh scent" on my hands. And it's all YOUR fault, Nikki!!

So after seeing that letter Brandon left on your locker, I did what any poor girl would do who was suffering from a very severe case of Post-Detention Stress Syndrome. . . .

ME, STEALING YOUR LETTER
DUE TO POST-DETENTION
STRESS SYNDROME

Anyway, while we were in class listening
to our bio teacher ramble on and on about,
um . . . ???

Actually, I don't have the SLIGHTEST idea
what that stupid teacher was rambling about.
I didn't hear a single word she said because
I was totally distracted READING the letter
Brandon wrote to you.

OMG! It was so DISGUSTINGLY sweet, sincere,
and apologetic, I almost threw up the tofu
burger I'd eaten for lunch!

It was very difficult for me to sit in class
and watch you and Brandon act like two
LOVESICK little LOVEBIRDS!

He stared at you the ENTIRE time, wondering
if you'd read his letter.

But, of course, you just totally IGNORED him
like he was a huge WAD OF GUM someone had
chewed and then stuck under your desk.

ME, READING BRANDON'S LETTER WHILE HE STARES AT YOU AND YOU TOTALLY IGNORE HIM!!

OMG! The entire situation made me so ANGRY and FRUSTRATED that I wanted to . . .

SCREEEEEEEEAM!! 😡!!!

But of course I couldn't, because then I would have gotten ANOTHER detention! And Principal Winston would have forced me to clean those nasty showers AGAIN ☹!!

EXCUSE ME! But I'm STILL suffering from a very severe case of Post-Detention Stress Syndrome from my LAST detention, which was all YOUR fault!

Anyway, Nikki, the good news is that everything worked out just as I had planned!! YAY ME ☺!!

Brandon was so desperate to make up with you that he followed every last detail of my Miss Know-It-All advice letter!

And because you never got the letter he left for you on your locker . . .

HE PATIENTLY WAITED FOR YOU AT
THE CUPCAKERY FOR TWO HOURS,
AND YOU NEVER SHOWED UP!

When Brandon finally gave up and left, he looked absolutely MISERABLE.

I felt SO sorry for the poor guy!

It was quite obvious he was DEVASTATED.

Probably because my Miss Know-It-All advice letter stated that if his friend (YOU!) didn't bother to show up at the CupCakery after getting his letter, it meant . . .

1. She was SO over him! Or . . .

2. She NEVER really cared about him to begin with.

Yes, I know!! You never GOT his letter!

OOPS!! MY BAD ☺!!

Sorry I'm NOT sorry!

But don't worry, Nikki.

The hurt and anger he's feeling right now won't last forever.

And maybe one day he'll forgive you for ripping out his heart, tossing it in the dirt, and then stomping all over it with your dorky pink high-top sneakers.

TOODLES!

MacKenzie

MY MISS KNOW-IT-ALL
MEANEST LETTER OF THE DAY

Dear Miss Know-It-All,

Could a popular boy ever fall for a nerdy girl?
I have a huge crush on a boy in my chemistry
class, but we hang in different circles. His
friends are jocks and cheerleaders, and my
friends and I are in the chess club.

He's actually really nice and shares some of
my interests. But when his friends are around,
things just get awkward. They bully me and try to
convince him I'm a loser. Although he stands up
for me, I'm just afraid one day he'll believe them!

Yesterday he asked me if I wanted to study
with him at the library, and I almost DIED!
I think he likes me okay as a friend, but it
makes me wonder if he LIKE likes me! I really
want to believe it's true, but my friends are
skeptical. They say popular boys never date
outside their clique.

187

Are they right, or do you think I have
a chance?

—*Geek Girl*

* * * * * * * * * * * * * * *

Dear Geek Girl,

Are you kidding me?? Wake up and smell the
caramel macchiato! He's not interested in you,
Boo Boo!

You need to get your head out of your
Lord of the Rings book and learn that reality
and fantasy are two different things. Love is not
blind, and popular kids and nerds do NOT mix!
If they got along, we wouldn't need cliques! Can
you imagine how horrible the world would be
without them? Who would I make fun of?!

Anyway, your friends are right to burst your
bubble. Boys think you're gross! As for your
library date with your crush, he's just studying

with you to improve his grades. Lemme speak
in Nerdese so you understand: You're getting
played like a pawn in chess! #Checkmate!

Sorry, but there's no romance in your future. If
you're so smart, why couldn't you figure it out
on your own?! I have better things to do than
waste time on these stupid letters! Now if you'll
excuse me, I'm off to get a manicure.

Toodles!
Miss Know-It-All

Dear Nikki,

I am SO excited! Daddy will be returning home from his business trip tomorrow evening.

So I plan to ~~ask~~ BEG my parents to let me transfer to North Hampton Hills International Academy.

I arranged for Nelson to take me to the mall today to buy my new school uniform.

My problem was that I only had $293 left over from my $500 monthly clothing allowance ☹!! And I ALSO needed to buy a handbag, jewelry, and hair accessories to match.

So when Mom gave me $100 to babysit my bratty little sister, Amanda, while she went to the country club to brunch with friends, I decided NOT to have my usual hissy fit.

AMANDA AND ME, TAKING THE LIMO
TO THE MALL TO SHOP FOR
MY NEW SCHOOL UNIFORM!

We arrived at the mall and took the escalator down to the huge, upscale department store that sold school uniforms.

"I love, love, love shopping!!" Amanda squealed. "I'm gonna buy a Princess Sugar Plum purse!"

"No, you don't understand, Amanda! YOU'RE not shopping! I AM!" I corrected her.

"But I wanna shop TOO!" she said, stomping her foot angrily. "Or you'll be SORRY . . . !"

"Excuse me? WHAT are you going to do? Wet your pants?" I asked sarcastically.

That's when Amanda suddenly started breathing really hard, hiccupping, and twitching. Did I mention that my little sister is the QUEEN of kiddie tantrums?

As her shrill voice reverberated through the mall, everyone stopped what they were doing to STARE at us.

OMG! I was SO EMBARRASSED!!

"Amanda!" I hissed. "Shut up before they call security and kick us out of the mall!" But that only made her scream LOUDER!

Lucky for me, I knew exactly how to deal with the little BRAT! I grabbed her hand and rushed past the food court, Toy City, and Puppy Palace to KANDY KINGDOM playland. As soon as Amanda saw it, she stopped screaming and squealed with delight! Thank goodness for short attention spans!

"You can play here while I shop, Amanda. If you need me, I'll be right next door trying on clothes in those fitting rooms with the pink curtains," I said, pointing about twenty-five yards away. "And don't you dare leave playland. I'm going to be keeping an eye on you from my dressing room."

"Okay, bye!" Amanda said, and ran off to join a group of kids on the slide.

Before you judge me for leaving Amanda at playland, put yourself in MY ~~shoes~~ heels.

How could I concentrate on finding the uniform and cute accessories with her screaming her bratty little head off like that?

I could NOT risk a fashion misstep, especially when I have a new school to impress.

Anyway, once inside the store, I discovered a ton of new summer arrivals!

I couldn't resist trying on just a few of them!

Before I knew it, my dressing room was overflowing with clothes.

It was hard to stop because I looked so FAB in EVERYTHING!

"Miss . . . I think you've tried on everything we have in the juniors, designer teens, prom gown, swimsuit, and shoe departments!" the exhausted sales assistant muttered. "Will you be purchasing any of these items today?"

"No thanks! That was just a try-on-a-thon!" I replied. "All I need is the North Hampton Hills school uniform. You can put all this stuff back!"

I don't know what the lady's problem was, but she started doing the same angry twitch thing that Amanda does.

"Of course, miss," she said through gritted teeth. "I'll go get my moving truck and be right back."

Note to self: Get her fired and sue the store!

Suddenly a disembodied head popped into my dressing room.

OMG! It almost SCARED the Mountain's Peak spring water out of me.

IT WAS AMANDA, RUDELY DROPPING
IN TO SHARE HER UNWANTED
FASHION ADVICE!!

"HELP!! It's a big, hairy RAT!" I screamed, and jumped onto a chair. "Oh! It's just you, Amanda. Sorry!"

"Well, I'M sorry YOU look like a PIG in lip gloss wearing a school uniform!" she snickered.

"Why don't you go back to Kandy Kingdom and accidentally fall off the slide?" I said, throwing a sock at her.

"I came to get a tissue for my snotty nose," Amanda sniffed. "I need to get one from your purse, okay?"

"Go right ahead. Just please stop BUGGING me!" I replied. "All this stress is giving me premature wrinkles!" I checked my face in the mirror and gushed. "False alarm. I'm STILL gorgeous!"

Amanda grabbed my purse and turned it upside down, dumping all my stuff onto the floor.

"Seriously?! WHAT are you doing?!!" I yelled.

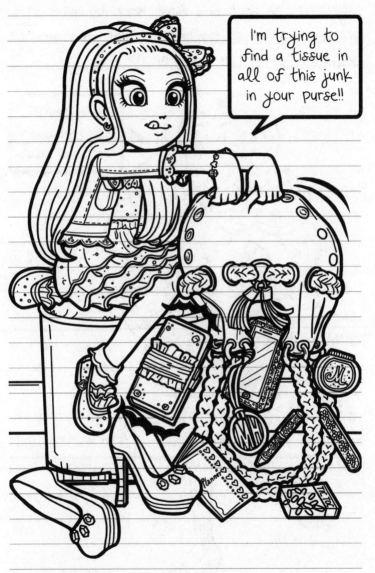

AMANDA, TRASHING MY PURSE!!

I ignored the brat and went back to admiring my new uniform in the mirror. There was no doubt about it! I was KILLIN' IT!!

Don't HATE me because I'm beautiful!

"Thanks, MacKenzie!" Amanda beamed as she gave me a big hug. "You're the BEST big sister EVER! I LOVE you! Have fun! Bye."

Now, that was a little odd. Amanda seemed REALLY thankful to get that tissue.

I found a leather-and-plaid purse that matched my skirt PERFECTLY! I also snagged the cutest jewelry and hair accessories! The best part was that everything was on sale.

YAY ME 😊!!

The saleslady at the register was super friendly. "My niece and nephew both go to North Hampton Hills. You're going to LOVE it there!" she said after I explained that I was transferring.

She wrapped all my items in tissue, placed them in a huge shopping bag, and then handed it to me.

"Okay, miss! Your total today is $357. Will that be cash or charge?"

"Cash, please," I said as I dug through my purse to retrieve my wallet. But for some reason, I couldn't find it. I giggled nervously at the saleslady and placed my purse on the counter. Then I very carefully looked through it again. Still no wallet.

In a panic, I turned it upside down and dumped it. Everything was there but my wallet. "OMG!" I finally cried. "I can't find my wallet!"

The saleslady gave me a dirty look and snatched the shopping bag from me like I was going to sneak out with it or something.

"I'll just hold on to THIS until you find your, um . . . lost wallet, or whatever," she sniffed.

"Excuse me? Seriously! My DAD could buy me a UNIFORM FACTORY if I wanted one!" I snapped at her.

The cashier glared at me. "Well, I don't know how your dad can buy you a factory if he can't afford to pay $357 for the items you were trying to take out of this store. I have a good mind to call SECURITY!"

Note to self: Get THIS lady fired along with that other lady. Then sue the store!

"Um, maybe it fell out in my dressing room?" I muttered as I started tossing stuff back into my purse.

When I grabbed a cold, soggy, USED tissue, I cringed. "GROSS!! How did that get in my—"

"OH. NO. SHE. DIDN'T!" I screamed as I rushed out of the store. "AMANDAAAAAA!!!!!"

Amanda was sitting inside the castle tower with a smug grin on her face.

"Amanda!!" I yelled. "Get your butt down here! NOW!"

As she slowly climbed down I noticed that she was carrying a large, blinged-out duffel bag.

"Give me back my wallet!" I screeched.

She zipped open a pocket on her new bag, took out my wallet, and threw it at me.

"If you weren't my sister, I'd have you arrested! And where did you get the money for that thing? You better tell me that you broke into your piggy bank. Again!"

Amanda folded her arms and glared at me.

I opened my wallet and stared at it in shock. All that was left was three dollars!

"OMG! Amanda, I can't believe you STOLE my wallet and SPENT all of my money!! You bratty little . . . THIEF!!"

"I borrowed it! I'll just pay you back on my next birthday when people give me lots of money." She shrugged. "Or I could always get some cash by selling my Barbie doll collection on eBay! Again!"

"Your birthday is ten months from now!" I yelled. "I need to pay for my uniform TODAY!"

"But, MacKenzie, just look at my fabulous purse!" she said, pointing to it. "What do you think? Do you love it, or do you LOOOVE it?!"

"Even though I admire your sophisticated taste in fake Italian handbags, which you obviously inherited from me, you're in SO much trouble right now!" I snarled. "Here's my wallet! You're going to return your bag, get a refund, and put my money BACK inside it. Or I'll tell Daddy what you did and he'll ground you until your tenth birthday! Do you understand me?!"

"YIP!"

I frowned at her. "WHAT?! Was that a yes?"

"No! Um . . . I mean . . . yes!" Amanda stammered.

"Yip! Yip!"

I narrowed my eyes at her.

"Actually, sometimes I make strange sounds when I'm nervous," she explained. "'Yip' means 'yes.' So, yip, I understand!"

"Yip-Yip! Yip!"

I heard it again. Only this time I knew it wasn't her. It actually seemed to be coming from her new purse.

"Um . . . Yip! Yip! Yip!" Amanda barked as her bag started to move.

Suddenly the flap opened and a white furball crawled out and wagged its tail.

AMANDA IS SO BUSTED!!

"OMG! A REAL puppy?" I exclaimed. "Amanda, WHY is there a PUPPY in your bag?!"

"Because all the girls at school are getting a puppy-in-a-purse! So I wanted one too!"

"But, Amanda, we ALREADY have a dog! You can just put Fifi in a purse!"

Of course I made Amanda take that puppy and pet carrier back to Puppy Palace to get a full refund. And boy, was she mad!

We were passing the toy store when Amanda went into another full-blown temper tantrum. I just grabbed her arm and tried to drag her toward the department store so I could pay for my uniform and get the heck out of there.

And yes! It was SOOO embarrassing! But I just totally IGNORED her!

Until she started screaming hysterically.

"STRANGER DANGER! SOMEONE PLEASE HELP ME!! I'M BEING KIDNAPPED!!"

That's when everyone in the mall turned around and started glaring at me all suspicious-like. I plastered a fake smile on my face and gave Amanda a little hug. "Just calm down, hon!" Then I whispered into her ear, "You spoiled little BRAT!! You better SHUT UP or else!"

"But I want my puppy-in-a-purse! NOOOW!!"

"Sorry! It's NOT happening! I don't have enough to pay for my uniform and a puppy!"

That's when Amanda fell on the floor and started writhing around like a SNAKE. "Get away from me, you KIDNAPPER! HELP! HELP! I'm being KIDNAPPED! Someone call the cops!"

If I got arrested, it could totally RUIN my chances of getting into North Hampton Hills! Lucky for me, I noticed a clearance TOY sale! I quickly offered Amanda a nice bribe if she'd stop screaming long enough for me to pay for my uniform and stuff. She accepted ☺!!

ME, WITH MY NEW SCHOOL
UNIFORM, AND AMANDA, WITH HER
NEW TOY-PUPPY-IN-A-PURSE

In spite of all the drama with Amanda, I'm finally all set for my first day of school at North Hampton Hills International Academy!

I just LOVE my new uniform!

And I'm going to look absolutely FABULOUS!!

YAY ME ☺!!

TOODLES!

MacKenzie ♡

MY MISS KNOW-IT-ALL
MEANEST LETTERS OF THE DAY

Today I have TWO letters:

* * * * * * * * * * * * * * *

Dear Miss Know-It-All,

There is a guy at school who I like. He is an athlete, very cute, cool, and popular. When we are alone he is super nice. But when he is with his friends, he acts like I don't exist. Is he really into me?

Thanks,
Invisible Girl

* * * * * * * * * * * * * * *

Dear Invisible Girl,

If this guy is a CCP, he is obviously out of your league!

213

He may ignore you when he is with his friends because he is ashamed of you. Guys like him want a smart, beautiful, and rich trophy girlfriend.

I'm sure he is just using you because you are smart and helping him with his homework. Or he's always really hungry and you let him eat the best stuff off your lunch tray every day.

My advice to you is to send me his photo and name because he sounds like my type and we could have a lot in common!

YAY ME!! 🙂!!

—Miss Know-It-All

* * * * * * * * * * * * * * * * *

I'm VERY sure this next letter is from my backstabbing ex-BFF, Jessica.

* * * * * * * * * * * * * * * *

Dear Miss Know-It-All,

I have a major BFF problem! Okay, so if I choose
popularity over my BFF and toss her out of
my life like a piece of moldy, two-week-old
pepperoni pizza, does that really make me a
bad person? I still secretly adore her, I just don't
want to be seen with her in public anymore.

She used to be queen of the CCPs. And when
she chose me over all the other girls in school
to be her BFF, my coolness factor instantly
increased from 6 to 100! I gained lots of cool
friends, invites to all the hottest parties, and
access to her penthouse-sized SHOE CLOSET!!!
I felt like I'd won the BFF lottery!

Then suddenly things changed! Popularity is
as fickle as shoe trends—one day it's all about
open-toed booties, and a week later they're out of
style and everyone is rocking diamond-encrusted
ballet flats. Well, the same thing happened with
my bestie. She made one little slip-up! And
suddenly she's LESS popular than a pair of ugly,

scuffed-up plastic rain boots at a designer shoe
sale. She has lost the special quality that made
me want to become her BFF in the first place.

Now the CCPs are looking for the next It Girl,
and this is finally MY chance to be the girl
everyone envies and wants to be. But hanging
out with my BFF could make ME as unpopular
as she is. I'm even having second thoughts
about inviting her to my upcoming birthday
bash at the country club.

So should I dump my BFF and pursue my dream
of becoming the next CCP Queen Bee (and
just live with the guilt)? Or should I be the loyal
friend who sticks by ~~MacKen~~ my BFF (even
though she's a complete embarrassment) and
give up the opportunity to finally have any
REAL happiness in my life?

—*CCP Princess*

* * * * * * * * * * * * * *

Dear CCP Princess,

Excuse me?! You REALLY should be thankful your AMAZING BFF allowed you to stuff your stinky, SASQUATCH-sized FEET into her designer stilettos!

Seriously, she DIDN'T have to be nice and show PITY to an unpopular WANNABE like YOU! You're lucky she didn't put you on blast when you showed up at Justin's party in that hideous, fluorescent-orange dress your (obviously senile) grandma made for you.

And was that crusty lime-green BOOGER in your nose supposed to be your statement accessory? Or didn't you see that massive, beach-ball-sized thing dangling in the wind when you looked in the mirror? Instead, your very loyal BFF rushed home and returned with a super-cute designer dress for you to wear at the party AND a tissue for that humongous booger.

217

You should be happy your BFF didn't dump you as her BFF when she caught you pretending to be her online just to chat with cute guys! I get it—you want to be her SO BADLY because you can't get a hungry, UGLY dude to look at you even with a FREE bologna sandwich tied around your neck.

Your BFF also could've told everyone your deepest, darkest secrets, like the fact that you wet the bed until you were ELEVEN YEARS OLD! Instead, she upgraded you from a frumpy NOBODY to a CCP socialite, and THIS is how you repay her generosity?! By stabbing her in the back so YOU can become the new CCP queen?!

Sorry! But you'll NEVER, EVER steal her crown as the smartest, prettiest, and fiercest diva of them all! So do yourself a big favor and don't waste your time trying! And don't let me catch you talking mess behind ~~my~~ your BFF's back again!

—*Miss Know-It-All*

Dear Nikki,

I'm sure you've already heard all the gossip about me and my BFF, Jessica. Well, I should say my EX-BFF, Jessica.

Ever since I caught her and my CCP friends making fun of me in that video, I have been so ANGRY that I could just . . .

SCREEEEEEEEAM! 😠!!

And then Jessica had the NERVE to actually write that letter to Miss Know-It-All TRASHING me like that!

Like, WHO does that kind of thing to another person?!

Well, okay! I'll admit that maybe I do those kinds of things to other people.

But definitely NOT to my BEST friend!!

I was in the girls' bathroom, just minding my own business and putting on a new layer of lip gloss. That's when Jessica came strutting in with some other CCP girls. I could NOT believe she actually had the nerve to ROLL her eyes at me like that.

So I was like, "Jessica! Excuse me, but I really DIDN'T appreciate you making fun of me in that video. But HATERS ARE GONNA HATE!"

And she was like, "MacKenzie, seriously! I have no idea what you are talking about!"

And I was like, "Oh, really! Well, I heard you've been talking trash behind my back just so you can take over my throne as Queen Bee!"

Then it got really, really quiet, and all the CCP girls were just staring at Jessica, waiting to see what lame excuse she was going to give for viciously stabbing me in the back like that.

And Jessica was like, "MacKenzie, I CAN'T EVEN . . . !!"

I could NOT believe she actually said that to me! So I told her off.

ME, TELLING JESSICA OFF
IN THE GIRLS' BATHROOM!!

Right now I'm so OVER Jessica!! I've already unfriended her butt on Facebook. I don't even care if I'm NOT invited to her stupid birthday party!

Anyway, if all of THAT wasn't enough DRAMA for one day, I was forced to watch part two in bio.

It was very obvious that you and Brandon were still upset with each other in class today. He was completely ignoring YOU, just like you were completely ignoring HIM.

That's when I decided to take matters into my own hands.

Maybe if you actually READ Brandon's letter, I wouldn't be forced to sit there and watch the two of you giving each other the cold shoulder.

So after bio today, I took responsibility for my actions and did the right thing!

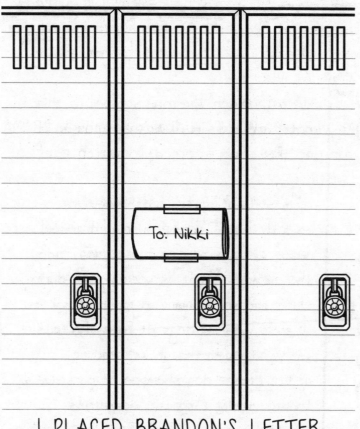

I PLACED BRANDON'S LETTER
BACK ON YOUR LOCKER ☺!

I was just hanging out at my locker, writing
in ~~your~~ MY diary when I saw you stop, stare
at his letter in surprise, and then quickly
open it:

Hi Nikki,

It's Brandon. Before you ball up this
note and toss it away, please read it
to the end.

I'm still not sure what happened
exactly, but I've been really bummed
since we quit hanging out. Biology isn't
the same without us goofing off during
class and you laughing at my lame jokes.
I miss washing dogs at Fuzzy Friends
with you, even though we end up
getting more dog shampoo on ourselves
than on them. And the dogs miss
you too!

Was it because of that . . . um, well,
what we did at the kissing booth, at
the end of the party? And the rumor
that came out afterward? I'm sorry
if I made you feel bad. I definitely

224

wish I hadn't done anything to mess up our friendship.

You said something about how you don't even know me. So what if we meet at the CupCakery after school today and grab some red velvet cupcakes—my treat! I'll tell you anything you want to know about me (and not worry that you'll think I'm weird). I've learned that honesty and trust are vital in a true friendship.

If you decide NOT to hang out today, I totally understand. I guess that will mean I don't really deserve your friendship. But it would make me happy if you would please give me another chance.

Your Fuzzy Friend,
Brandon

OMG, Nikki! After you read that letter, you were SO happy you went "SQUEEEEEE!!" like a little mouse! Then you started giggling and doing a very weird dance right there in the hall.

You texted the news to Chloe and Zoey, and they ran up, screaming their heads off like you were Taylor Swift or somebody.

Then the three of you did a group hug!

I was a little confused when I overheard you guys planning to meet at your house after school to pick out what you were going to wear.

Then, after you left, I FINALLY realized that you thought you were supposed to meet Brandon after school . . . TODAY!!

I'll admit the mix-up was partly MY fault!

Seriously, Nikki, I could NOT believe . . .

226

← ME

YOU PATIENTLY WAITED FOR BRANDON
AT THE CUPCAKERY FOR TWO HOURS
AND HE NEVER SHOWED UP!

I don't blame you one bit for being even more FURIOUS with him for standing you up like that! Especially after he wrote you that very sappy letter pouring his heart out to you.

I understand why you feel more CONFUSED than a CHAMELEON in a bag of SKITTLES! Your relationship with Brandon is DOOMED! And it's NEVER, EVER going to work out ☹!

YAY ME ☺!! Sorry I'm NOT sorry!

Anyway, even though you're very disappointed that you and Brandon are SO over, please don't throw a huge pity party for yourself.

Some people have WAY more serious problems than you do! And by "people," I mean girls like ME ☹!!

Right now I'm so MAD at my PARENTS I could just . . .

SCREEEEEEEEEEAM!! 😠!

After dinner I tried to have a heart-to-heart talk with my parents about me transferring to North Hampton Hills International Academy!

And as usual they were practically IGNORING every word I said. Daddy was reading the newspaper. And Mommy was checking her hair and applying, like, her ninth layer of lipstick (she's ADDICTED to lipstick).

And in case you were wondering, Amanda was upstairs having a temper tantrum. WHY?! Because when she was potty training her new toy puppy, she accidentally DROPPED it, and clogged the TOILET!

Yes, I know!! That child has SERIOUS issues!!

Anyway, I begged, I screamed, and I cried.

I put on such a theatrical performance that I should receive an Academy Award nomination for Most Dramatic Meltdown in a Family Convo.

229

ME, HAVING A COMPLETE
EMOTIONAL MELTDOWN WHILE
MY PARENTS CALMLY IGNORE ME!!

I was like, "Mommy! Daddy! You don't understand. The kids at my school HATE me!! Every day I see them watching that video of me with that bug in my hair! And they LAUGH and make fun of me like I'm an UNPOPULAR person or something!"

"Honey, it can't be THAT bad! Just last week you were saying how many friends you have and how much you LOVE your school! The kids just think it's a harmless little joke. I'm sure they don't mean to upset you," my mom said.

"Yes, they DO! Going there every day and dealing with that video is TORTURE! I need to transfer to North Hampton Hills International Academy ASAP! Like tomorrow! PLEEEEASE!"

"Now, MacKenzie, just calm down. It's only a silly little video that kids are passing around on their phones. And by tomorrow they'll probably be watching something else," my dad said sternly.

"But it's RUINING my LIFE!" I sobbed hysterically.

"No, it's NOT ruining your life!" my dad argued. "Now, if this bully, Nicholas, had . . ."

"Dad! HER name is NIKKI!" I screamed.

"Okay . . . NIKKI, then! Now, if this bully, Nikki, had posted the video online, it would be a completely different situation. Then we'd know for sure she had hostile intentions. I wouldn't consider it just a harmless little prank."

"She's obviously upset, Marshall! Maybe we should set up a meeting with Principal Winston," my mom said, looking at her watch. "I have a meeting in twenty minutes about our annual fund-raiser for the children's hospital. So we'll finish this discussion later, MacKenzie, dear. Nelson is already waiting for me in the car," she said as she kissed my forehead. "Toodles!"

"But, MOM!" I groaned. "Please! Don't leave!"

"Okay, so here's the plan," my dad said as he turned to the stock market page and frowned at the numbers. "Let's give it another month. If things don't improve by then, we'll schedule a little chat with your principal to get to the bottom of this."

"BUT WHAT AM I SUPPOSED TO DO UNTIL THEN?!" I shrieked at the top of my lungs.

That's when both of my parents looked at each other nervously and said four little words. And NO! Those words weren't "YES, you can transfer!"

They said, "LET'S CALL DR. HADLEY!"

I was like, "EXCUSE ME!! SORRY! But I don't NEED a therapy session right now!!"

If I wanted ADVICE on how to deal with my problems, I'd just write Miss Know-It-All, hack into the website, and send a response to MYSELF!!

"What I NEED is for you to enroll me at North Hampton Hills International Academy! NOW!"

OMG! I was so FURIOUS with my parents.

That's when I totally lost it and screamed ...

ME, TOTALLY LOSING IT AND YELLING AT MY PARENTS!!

Then I ran upstairs to my room and slammed the door!

SERIOUSLY! My parents are such IDIOTS!!

They expect me to stay at WCD and ROT while the kids there laugh at me every day like I'm some kind of unpopular LOSER!!

I CAN'T EVEN . . . !!!

HOW CAN MY VERY OWN PARENTS ACTUALLY BELIEVE THIS VIDEO ISN'T A SERIOUS PROBLEM UNTIL SOME HATER POSTS IT ONLINE??!!!

Well, Mommy and Daddy!!!

Guess what?!

THAT can be easily ARRANGED!! . . .

ME, CYBERBULLYING MYSELF BY
POSTING MY OWN VIDEO ONLINE!

Now that my imaginary cyberbully has placed that disgusting video online, my parents will feel SO SORRY for me that they'll FINALLY let me transfer!!

YAY ME ☺!!

North Hampton Hills International Academy, here I COME!!!

TOODLES!

♡Mackenzie♡

MY MISS KNOW-IT-ALL
MEANEST LETTER OF THE DAY

I'm pretty sure this next letter is from Marcy, that shy and very strange little friend of yours. She has BRACES, right?!

* * * * * * * * * * * * * *

Dear Miss Know-It-All,

I haven't been my normal, happy self since I was told I needed to get braces.

I'm embarrassed to say this, but when my orthodontist gave me the news, I burst into tears right there in the chair. The truth is, I'm already insecure and this whole braces fiasco is just making me feel a lot worse.

Now whenever I look in the mirror, I imagine an ugly freak with barbed-wire teeth staring back at me. It's a big struggle to get through the school day without crying.

I'm sure you've heard all the horror stories about kids with braces being relentlessly teased and called cruel names. Why do people have to kick a girl when she's already down??

I feel frustrated, depressed, and alone. I haven't told my friends about any of this because lately they've been dealing with problems of their own.

But I know you're the perfect person to give me the encouragement and advice that I need to get through this! Please help!

—*Blue in Braces*

* * * * * * * * * * * * * * * *

Since this girl (Marcy?) sounds like a complete BASKET CASE, I plan to e-mail her my advice tomorrow.

WARNING: This letter is so MEAN, it's probably worth at least a three-day detention! Sorry, Nikki ☺!

* * * * * * * * * * * * * * *

Dear Brace Face,

Did I get your name right? Or was it
Zipper Mouth? Maybe it was STUMP GRINDER!
Sorry, sweetie. I'm so forgetful sometimes!
Anyway, having braces isn't all that bad.
Let's look at the pros and cons, shall we?

PROS:
#1: You can get a job at the Olive Garden
restaurant grating cheese with your teeth!

#2: Your mouth also multitasks as a paper
shredder and chain saw!

#3: With all the food you're going to have stuck
in your braces, you'll have yourself a portable,
FREE all-you-can-eat buffet!

CONS:
#1: People will follow you around to get a better
cell phone signal.

240

#2: A boyfriend with braces could become the kiss of death, literally. If your braces lock up during a smooch, you'll both have to go to the orthodontist together to get it surgically terminated!

#3: On a very clear day, you can pick up interstellar signals from ALIENS on Mars!

Wait a second!! ALL of those sound like CONS, don't they?

Oh well! Too bad for you!

Thank goodness I've ALWAYS had perfectly straight pearly whites!

YAY ME 😊!!

—Miss Know-It-All

TUESDAY, APRIL 22

Dear Nikki,

I thought this moment would never come!

Today is my FINAL DAY at Westchester Country Day Middle School ☺!!

YAY ME ☺!!

Everything worked out just as I had planned.

My parents saw that video of me on the Internet that was posted by that HORRIBLE BULLY at my school.

Namely, YOU!

I was so upset by what you did that I cried myself to sleep last night.

My parents felt SO sorry for me!

So first thing this morning they contacted North Hampton Hills International Academy and arranged for my transfer. YAY ME 😊!!

I totally impressed the headmaster at my admissions interview. She actually said I'd be an asset to their academic institution.

So on Thursday I take the placement tests for all my classes.

As I'm writing this Mommy and Daddy are in the WCD office finalizing paperwork and I'm cleaning out my locker and packing up my personal belongings.

Well, actually, I'm supervising the mover guy.

When I leave, I KNOW you and your BFFs will be standing in the hall rudely STARING at me and wondering what's going on.

But I'll just IGNORE you like I always do! . . .

ME, LEAVING WCD TO ATTEND
NORTH HAMPTON HILLS
INTERNATIONAL ACADEMY ☺!!

And yes! I know there will be a lot of unanswered questions about my sudden departure. But please don't believe any nasty rumors.

The truth is, I'll probably be in Hawaii, on a ninety-foot yacht, wearing a super-cute designer sundress with matching sandals, sipping on a pineapple-mango smoothie, while working on my "Volcanoes in Hawaii" report with the very smart, rich, and posh students in my study group from North Hampton Hills International Academy!!

YAY ME!! ☺!!

Did I mention that most of the students there are the children of celebs, politicians, business tycoons, and royalty?!

I almost forgot to mention that there's been a slight change in plans regarding your diary.

First, I'm totally addicted to writing in it!

And second, I think your diary entries should be shared with the entire WORLD!

Also, don't forget that my final GIFT will be delivered to you on Monday, April 28.

After you're EXPELLED from WCD for cyberbullying, you're going to need a new school too!

And whatever you do, PLEASE, PLEASE, PLEASE don't transfer to North Hampton Hills International Academy ☺!

TOODLES!

MacKenzie

P.S. I left you a little good-bye note and stuck it on my old locker!

MY MISS KNOW-IT-ALL
MEANEST LETTER OF THE DAY

Unfortunately, with the transfer and all, today was way too hectic for me to answer any advice letters.

And since I'm going to be super busy at my new school with all my new friends, you can consider this my official RESIGNATION!

I really enjoyed being Miss Know-It-All! Saving a few hopeless weirdos from themselves was a lot like charity work. But most important, it made ME feel all warm and fuzzy inside!

I honestly think this whole experience has changed my life for the better and made me a nicer, more compassionate person.

NOT!!

!!

OMG!
YOU'LL NEVER
BELIEVE
WHAT
HAPPENED
TO ME
YESTERDAY!!

RING
RING
RING!!

253

258

I FINALLY FOUND MY DIARY!! SQUEEEEE ☺!!

I'M SO HAPPY RIGHT NOW, I THINK I'M GOING TO GIVE IT A BIG FAT . . .

← KISS!

It's been missing for

TWO. WHOLE. WEEKS!!!

And the entire time, I've been an emotional

WRECK!!

My BFFs and I looked EVERYWHERE for it!
I had pretty much given up hope of EVER finding
my diary again.

And poor Zoey blamed herself for losing it!
She thought it had somehow fallen out when she'd
gone into my backpack to get some gum.

I told her that even if it had, it was totally
an accident and I wasn't mad at her.

But Zoey STILL felt responsible and insisted
that she was the Worst. Friend. EVER!

She'd been moping around, like, FOREVER, and Chloe and I have been worried about her.

But when I showed Zoey my diary, she was so happy she actually burst into tears of joy!

Now I have my diary AND my BFF Zoey back ☺!

SQUEEEEE!!

The WEIRDEST part is that my diary looked completely different when I found it.

The SNEAKY DIARY SNATCHER had given it a SUPERcute MAKEOVER with a FAB new LEOPARD print cover!

It looked exactly like an expensive designer blouse that I'd seen at the mall for $220!

The day my diary disappeared, I had my suspicions. I wanted to plaster posters of my PRIME SUSPECT all over the school. . . .

WANTED!!

MACKENZIE HOLLISTER,
FOR THEFT OF DIARY
(WARNING: Cute but dangerous!)

But, unfortunately, I didn't have any proof she was the
STICKY-FINGERED SCOUNDREL who'd stolen it.

Anyway, I could NOT believe all the stuff MacKenzie wrote in MY diary!

I stayed up past midnight and read every last entry. TWICE! She actually gave me a glimpse into her brain.

In spite of her beauty and popularity, her life is not nearly as perfect as everyone thinks.

She just pretends that it is.

And yes, I know MacKenzie is stressed out from all the drama in her life including (1) the detention, (2) the bug video, (3) losing her BFF, Jessica, (4) her insane jealousy of my friendship with Brandon, and (5) wanting to transfer to a new school.

But STILL!! As my grandmother always says, "Everything happens for a reason. And sometimes that reason is you make BAD choices!"

MacKenzie creates a lot of her own problems and then blames them on others.

However, the most SHOCKING thing I discovered was just how DIABOLICAL she is.

HOW diabolical IS she?!

When life gives her LEMONS, she squeezes the juice in other people's EYES!! I'm just sayin'.

I'd actually feel sorry for her if she wasn't so CRUEL.

Anyway, this thing gets even more UNBELIEVABLE!

MacKenzie found my user ID and password in one of MY earlier diary entries and BROKE into my Miss Know-It-All website ☹!!

I'm so NOT lying!!

Then she wrote a bunch of MEAN and NASTY advice letters to unsuspecting students.

Her plan was to get ME kicked out of school for CYBERBULLYING!!

Like, WHO does that?!!!

Thankfully, my Miss Know-It-All newspaper column doesn't publish until Monday, April 28, so I have plenty of time to fix any damage she's done and delete her letters.

In spite of that, I'm STILL a little worried about her THREAT that she has a SURPRISE for me on Monday, April 28 ☹!

But here's the most SHOCKING news of all!!

MACKENIZE HOLLISTER TRANSFERRED TO A NEW SCHOOL!

And yesterday was her last day at WCD!

YES! I know it's really hard to believe! But it's TRUE!! The entire school is GOSSIPING about it, even the teachers.

That DRAMA QUEEN is actually gone from my life!! FOREVER!! WOO-HOO!! . . .

ME, DOING MY SNOOPY HAPPY DANCE
BECAUSE MACKENZIE IS GONE!!

Since MacKenzie is out of the way, I can
FINALLY try to patch things up with Brandon
without HER interfering ☺!

He's been SUPERbusy lately, doing photography for
both the newspaper and yearbook.

We've basically ignored each other and have barely
spoken since that big blowup at my locker a few
weeks ago.

Then things went from bad to worse after
Brandon wrote that really sweet apology letter
inviting me to hang out with him at the CupCakery.

I waited there for him, like, FOREVER, but he never showed up ☹!

I was mad at HIM because I thought he'd stood me up since HE was still mad at ME. And yes! I know it sounds crazy.

But according to MacKenzie's diary entries, SHE was behind the scenes, MANIPULATING everyone and creating all the DRAMA.

I have to admit, I've really missed Brandon these past few weeks. I need to talk to him tomorrow and apologize for everything that's happened.

Anyway, now that MacKenzie has transferred to a new school, my life at WCD is FINALLY going to be DRAMA FREE and absolutely PERFECT!!

SQUEEEEEE!!

!!

NOTE TO SELF:

Chloe wasn't in school yesterday or today, and she hasn't answered any of my text messages.

Which is very STRANGE!

Hopefully, Zoey has heard from her!

But if NOT . . .

1. Call Chloe tonight to make sure she's okay!!

2. Tell her the FANTASTIC news that I FINALLY found my diary ☺!!

3. Let her know that we don't have to worry about Zoey anymore because she's back to her normal happy self. SQUEEE!!

ALSO:

Don't forget to explain everything to Brandon and apologize!

FRIDAY, APRIL 25

AAAAAHHHHH ☹!!!

(That was me screaming!)

I thought things would be a lot better with MacKenzie gone.

But today is turning out to be the WORST day EVER!!

I'd already made up my mind that if Chloe was absent again today, Zoey and I were going to stop by her house after school.

The two of us had been calling, texting, and e-mailing Chloe almost nonstop since Wednesday, but we hadn't heard anything from her.

Not even a PEEP!!

What's up with THAT?!!

First Zoey was acting strange, and now Chloe?! JUST GREAT ☹!!

I was worried that something BAD had happened to Chloe on her way to school on Wednesday.

You know, like maybe she got kidnapped by some teen zombies. And they were holding her hostage because they wanted to make her their teen zombie QUEEN.

YIKES ☹!!

Hey, it could happen!

We FINALLY spotted Chloe coming out of the office after second period, Zoey and I were SUPERhappy and nearly HYSTERICAL.

We ran right up to her and shrieked, "Chloe! Chloe! OMG! WHERE have you been?! We tried to contact you! Didn't you get any of our calls, e-mails, or texts?! Are you okay?! Were you sick? We really missed you! Guess what?! We've been DYING to tell you the big news! WE FOUND THE DIARY!!! SQUEEEEE!!"

But then the strangest thing happened! . . .

SHE JUST ROLLED HER EYES AT US
AND WALKED AWAY!

We stood there in shock, staring at our BFF with our mouths hanging open!

Chloe acted like we weren't even there. I could NOT believe she just totally DISSED us like that.

Zoey and I were hurt and confused! But more than anything, we were frustrated by all the unanswered questions.

Why hadn't Chloe bothered to return our millions of phone calls, texts, and e-mails?

What was she upset about?

Why had she been absent?

Was she mad at US?

And if so, why?

But we never got a chance to ask her anything because she SULKED during gym class and was so GLUM at lunch that she refused to even talk to us.

However, Zoey and I were DETERMINED. We were NOT about to give up on our BFF.

So we made a SECRET PLAN.

Later in the day, when the three of us worked in the library together as shelving assistants, we'd be SUPERnice and kind to Chloe to cheer her up.

Then, once she was in a better mood, we'd get her to open up and talk to us about what was bothering her.

And by the end of the hour we'd do a group hug and be BFFs once again. SQUEEEEE!!

More very soon . . . !!

☺!!!
...

When I left off, Zoey and I were about to implement our secret plan to resolve the CHLOE CRISIS.

"Are you guys as bored as I am?" I muttered, dusting the clean library tables again just to stay awake.

"Well, we could always erase pencil marks from the dictionaries," Zoey suggested.

"I'm not THAT bored!" I grumped. "Do you have any ideas, Chloe?"

Zoey and I looked at her hopefully. But she stared straight ahead and didn't say a word.

"Chloe, what's up? You've been SUPERquiet all day. Is anything wrong?" Zoey asked.

Chloe bit her lip and shook her head no.

"I have an idea. Since we're bored silly, let's play Chloe's favorite game!" I exclaimed. "Charades!"

"That sounds like fun!" Zoey agreed.

"And it beats erasing pencil marks out of dictionaries any day," I said. "Chloe, you can go first."

Chloe folded her arms and just stood there with an unamused look on her face.

"Hmm . . . ," I said, scratching my head. "No movement and blank stare. You're a . . . ROCK?"

Chloe scowled at me and shook her head.

"Well, how about a TREE?" Zoey guessed.

Chloe rolled her eyes for the tenth time today and stood perfectly still. That's when a creative guess popped into my head.

"I know! You're a very ANGRY STATUE?!" I exclaimed. "Right?!"

WRONG!! Chloe gave me an icy stare that was so cold, I almost got frostbite! OUCH!! . . .

CHLOE, GIVING ME AN ICY STARE
DURING OUR FUN GAME OF CHARADES!

I think my very creative guess must have ticked Chloe off or something, because she clenched her fists and stormed across the room.

"Wait! Where are you going?" I called after her. "Zoey and I haven't had our turns yet!"

Chloe shot me a dirty look and violently slammed the library door behind her. BAM!!!

"What just happened?" I asked, totally confused. "Did I miss something?"

"I think we both did," Zoey answered solemnly. "Chloe is obviously angry and giving us both the silent treatment!"

"But why?!" I asked, flabbergasted. "What did we say or do to make her so upset?"

"I don't have the slightest idea!" Zoey shrugged. "She's usually so sweet and bubbly. Maybe she's just having a bad day."

"It feels more like a bad WEEK!" I said with a sigh.

"Well, let's just back off and give her some space. Hopefully, she'll feel better tomorrow," Zoey said.

"If you say so. But it feels like she's HATING us MORE every minute," I complained.

Zoey shook her head and gave a long, sad sigh.

"We both need to be there for Chloe when she's ready to talk. Just remember . . . 'A friend is someone who knows the SONG in your HEART and can SING it back to you when you FORGET the WORDS!'—Author unknown."

OMG! That was the most kind, thoughtful, and sympathetic thing I'd ever heard.

Zoey is the BEST friend ever!

And when it comes to sorting out complicated emotions, she's like a teen Dr. Phil in sparkle lip gloss and skinny jeans.

We didn't have the slightest idea why Chloe was upset.

Because, unfortunately, our secret plan to cheer her up . . . DIDN'T.

Zoey and I left the library feeling more worried than EVER.

☹!!

The situation with Chloe was emotionally draining.

But it wasn't the ONLY DRAMAFEST I had to deal with on Friday.

The other one began when I discovered the cafeteria was serving what looked like deep-fried hockey pucks smothered in a diarrhea gravy.

And smelled like it too ☹! EWWW!!

So I decided to just have a banana for lunch.

I was obviously very distracted about the Chloe Crisis, because when I went to throw away my banana peel, I had a very unfortunate and slightly traumatic ACCIDENT ☹!

With this GUY!!

Only, it wasn't just ANY guy. . . .

ME, ACCIDENTALLY SMACKING
BRANDON WITH A BANANA PEEL!

I could NOT believe Brandon actually said that.

I NEVER, EVER said he was GARBAGE!!

Now, maybe I TREATED him like garbage ☹!

But I never actually CALLED him that.

BIG! DIFFERENCE!

After my apology crashed and burned, we just
stood there staring at each for what seemed like
FOREVER!

"So, Brandon, um . . . how are things going?"
I asked awkwardly, and plastered on a smile.

Brandon looked down at the slimy banana peel slowly
sliding down the front of his shirt, then looked back
at me and raised an eyebrow.

"OMG! SORRY! Let me take care of that for
you! Don't move!" I said as I dashed to the

nearest lunch table like my hair was on fire.

I snatched a fistful of napkins from a dispenser and rushed back to Brandon.

"I'll have you cleaned up in no time," I said, catching my breath.

I peeled the banana from his shirt and tossed it into a (real) garbage can. Then I dabbed at the slimy stain.

"Don't worry about it," Brandon said, looking rather embarrassed. "No big deal. You really don't have to—"

"Yes, I DO!" I interrupted. "Firstly, it was my fault. And secondly, I'm your FRIEND! Although, with everything that's happened lately, it probably doesn't seem like it," I admitted sheepishly.

"Friend? Really, Nikki?! You yelled at me for no apparent reason. Then, after I wrote you an apology letter, you stood me up. Sorry! But with friends like you, who needs enemies?!" he said, obviously a little ticked off at me.

"Actually, I didn't mean to yell at you! That day I spazzed out, MacKenzie was being a major pain, and I seriously thought YOU were HER when I said those things," I explained. "And I DID try to meet you at the CupCakery. But thanks to MacKenzie, I got there THREE days late! That girl is so hopelessly DERANGED, she actually SABOTAGED our relationship with red velvet CUPCAKES! Like, WHO does that?!" I ranted.

"So you're saying all of this is MacKenzie's fault? And she was trying to undermine our friendship again?" Brandon asked skeptically.

"Yes! That's exactly what I'm saying! It's at least partially her fault. Brandon, she's CRIMINALLY INSANE! She started that nasty pizza rumor about you! And I won't even tell you what she's done to me lately, because you'd never believe it. She needs to be locked up in a high-security UNDERGROUND PRISON. In CHAINS!" I fumed.

"Thank goodness she transferred to another school!"

"I'm sorry, Nikki . . . but after all this . . . DRAMA, I don't know what to believe anymore," Brandon said grimly. "Maybe I don't know YOU as well as I thought."

Well, THAT little comment sounded vaguely familiar.

I'd said the exact same thing to HIM during our last argument. I could NOT believe that dude was stealing MY lines!

Suddenly I noticed that the room seemed unusually quiet.

That's when I turned to see the ENTIRE cafeteria GAWKING at us. Like we were a scene from one of those overdramatic teen romance blockbuster movies.

OMG! I was SO embarrassed. . . .

ME, IN SHOCK TO DISCOVER THE ENTIRE
CAFETERIA GAWKING AT US!

As the bell rang signaling lunch was over, Brandon sighed and silently stared at me. He looked like he was deeply pondering everything I'd just said. Or trying to figure out who was more CUCKOO, me or MacKenzie!

"Nikki, honestly, I think we should just . . ." He hesitated and glanced at his watch.

I held my breath and prayed he would give our friendship another chance.

". . . I think we should just get to BIO before we're late. Are you coming?" he asked as he dumped his lunch tray.

That's when I totally PANICKED!

Did this mean our relationship was OVER?

Obviously, we WEREN'T girlfriend and boyfriend. And for the past few weeks we HADN'T even been very good FRIENDS.

So what exactly WAS our relationship?!

And why did it feel so overwhelming? And confusing? And exhilarating? And special? All at the same time.

Then it finally hit me! Maybe Brandon wanted to talk about things on our way to bio!

You know, privately. Without the entire cafeteria eavesdropping on our conversation.

How ROMANTIC would that be ☺?!!

I turned again to look at all the faces STILL staring at us.

Suddenly, I felt a TINY ray of hope! Maybe we could get our friendship back on track after all!

That's when I smiled and finally answered his question. "Um . . . OKAY! Let's get to class."

But when I turned around . . .

BRANDON WAS GONE!

I came to school early to do a complete review of my Miss Know-It-All letters and search for possible clues about that "surprise" MacKenzie had mentioned.

She had answered about a dozen letters and saved them to my "New Letters" file.

All letters are stored there until I e-mail my advice to students and/or place a copy in the "Auto-Publish" file, which automatically publishes my letters in the school newspaper every Monday at 12:30 p.m.

OMG! Her letters were SO cruel, I cringed just reading them.

And the bad news is that she'd ALREADY e-mailed her advice letters to three students ☹!

After reading about their problems, MacKenzie had guessed that "Massively Cruddy Friend" was

290

Brandon, "CCP Princess" was Jessica, and "Blue in Braces" was my friend Marcy.

The letter she sent Brandon had created a cupcake nightmare, but he'd managed to survive.

And that backstabbing WANNABE, Jessica, totally deserved the nasty letter her ex-BFF, MacKenzie, had sent her!

But I was a little worried about Marcy.

I made a mental note to talk to her and make sure she hadn't been traumatized by that awful letter she'd received from Miss Know-It-All.

I didn't have a choice but to explain it as a very bad joke and apologize for sending it to her.

I printed copies of MacKenzie's letters (just in case I ever needed them!) and then completely DELETED them from my "New Letters" file.

PROBLEM SOLVED ☺!

MacKenzie's Reign of Terror as the FAKE Miss Know-It-All was officially OVER!!

It was a big fat coincidence that Marcy just happened to walk into the newspaper office as I was finishing up.

And get this! She didn't seem upset at all!

As a matter of fact, she thanked me (again!) for the trip to New York City for National Library Week and gushed nonstop about what a BLAST it had been for Violet, Jenny, and her.

But here's the WEIRD part! When I tried to apologize for the advice letter from Miss Know-It-All about her braces, Marcy claimed she didn't have the slightest idea what I was talking about. She said she HADN'T written a letter to my advice column! Recently, anyway.

Marcy went on to say that her braces weren't so bad once she got used to them, AND she was happy and excited because they were FINALLY coming off in just THREE months!

Okay! THAT convo was really AWKWARD ☹!!

So, MacKenzie was wrong! It appeared that the "Blue in Braces" letter had been written by one of the other dozens of students with braces at our school. JUST GREAT ☹!!

I gathered my stuff and rushed off to meet Zoey at Chloe's locker with my fingers crossed that things would finally be back to normal.

But no such luck! Chloe slammed her locker and walked right past us without saying a word.

It was officially Day Four of the Chloe Crisis!

By lunchtime Zoey and I had come up with the brilliant idea to leave a note on Chloe's locker asking her to meet us in the janitor's closet during lunch to talk.

The three of us always met there when we wanted to discuss important stuff in private.

Zoey quickly scribbled a note from us. . . .

Dear Chloe,

What's wrong?! Are you mad at us? We've been super worried about you these past few days. Do you want to talk about it?

PLEASE, PLEASE, PLEASE meet us in the janitor's closet ASAP! We don't mean to bug you or anything. We just care about you because you're our BFF!!

ZOEY and NIKKI

P.S. We're really sad and miss you ☹!!

Then we folded our letter and taped it to Chloe's locker.

As the bell rang for lunch Zoey and I exchanged nervous glances and rushed off to set up camp in the janitor's closet.

We waited and waited, but it looked like Chloe was going to be a no-show.

That had NEVER, EVER happened before.

Almost overnight it seemed our BFF had turned into a BIGGER drama queen than MacKenzie.

Just as we were about to give up hope, the door clicked and slowly opened.

We were relieved to see Chloe standing there.

She looked really sad, and her eyes were red like she had been crying or something.

"Guys, I've got really bad news!" she said, sniffing.

Those were the first words she'd actually spoken to us in what seemed like a year!!

Zoey and I just stared at her silently.

I got a big lump in my throat, and my heart pounded so loudly I could hear it in my ears.

I was afraid Chloe was going to say her family was moving away to Timbuktu or somewhere!

OMG!

What would Zoey and I do without our BFF?!

I didn't even want to think about it ☹!

Chloe just stood there, kind of trembling like she was going to burst into tears.

Finally, she took a deep breath, pointed at her lips, and then slowly stretched them into what looked like a pink gloss-covered grimace.

"So, you refused to speak to us for all this time because you've been hating on your lip gloss color?!" I exclaimed in disbelief. "Really?!"

Zoey gave me a swift jab with her elbow and shot me a dirty look.

"OUCH!" I whimpered under my breath.

"Actually, we love that color on you, Chloe!" Zoey reassured her as she plastered a fake grin on her face. "It's SUPERcute! Right, Nikki?"

"Yeah, Zoey, REALLY cute! It's actually the same pinkish-red color as the BRUISE you just gave me. You know, before it swells and turns black, blue, and purple," I muttered.

Zoey shot me another dirty look.

"WHAT?!!" I shrugged at her.

Chloe gave us a massive eye roll.

Then she very dramatically showed us her clenched teeth.

Zoey and I could NOT believe our eyes. . . .

ZOEY AND ME, STARING AT CHLOE'S TEETH!

As we both leaned in for a closer look, Chloe smiled shyly (for the first time in days!) and blurted out . . .

"I JUST GOT BRACES!!"

I was so shocked and surprised, I had to restrain myself from TOTALLY freaking out! Chloe was ALREADY traumatized, and I didn't want to make her feel even WORSE.

As she stood there nervously smiling at us, it was quite obvious that Chloe looked ~~adorable~~ ADORKABLE in her new braces.

"OMG! You look SOOO cute in them," Zoey squealed, like she was admiring a new puppy.

"Wow!! Those hot-pink wires really bring out the warmth in your skin tone. And . . . um, the purple brackets complement your eye color!" I gushed, just like those annoying salesgirls at the mall.

Only, I really meant what I said. Kind of.

"Come on! You guys are just saying that to make me feel better!" Chloe sniffed. "Are you sure I don't look like a metal-mouthed . . . FREAK?!"

"Of course NOT!" I yelled.

"Girl, are you KA-RAY-ZEE?!" Zoey screamed.

That's when Zoey and I grabbed our BFF, gave her a big hug, and gushed . . .

CHLOE, YOU'RE BEAUTIFUL!!

ZOEY AND ME, GIVING CHLOE A BIG HUG!

Chloe explained that she was absent from school on Wednesday and Thursday because she was getting her braces. (And to think that I was worried that she had been kidnapped and forced to become a zombie queen!)

"Chloe, why didn't you just TELL us you were getting braces?!" I asked.

"Actually, I did! Kind of," she explained. "But I wanted your HONEST opinion. So I wrote in to your Miss Know-It-All column."

"Are you sure? I never got a letter from you," I answered, slightly confused.

"Well, actually, I didn't use my own name. I wrote in anonymously that I was freaking out about getting braces and asked you for advice. I signed my letter—"

"BLUE IN BRACES!" I practically screamed. "OMG, Chloe! That letter was from YOU?!"

"Yes! I got YOUR letter Tuesday morning, but I didn't get a chance to read it until after school. To be honest, Nikki, your letter made me feel a lot worse!!" Chloe sniffed. "It sounded like you HATED people with braces. That's why I kind of freaked out and stopped talking. I was afraid that if you found out about my braces, you guys wouldn't want to be my friend anymore."

Zoey scowled at me. I quickly scooted away from her, just in case she tried to elbow me again.

"OMG, Chloe! I am SO sorry!" I apologized as a wave of sadness washed over me. "I feel just AWFUL! You did NOT deserve that horrible letter! It probably won't make you feel any better, but . . . I DIDN'T write it!"

"WHAT?!" Chloe and Zoey gasped. "Then WHO did?!"

Up until now, I had been SUPERworried about Chloe and totally distracted by the problems with my Miss Know-It-All column. So this was actually the PERFECT time to finally tell Chloe and Zoey all the nitty-gritty details about MacKenzie.

Starting with the shocking fact that not only had she STOLEN my diary, but she had actually WRITTEN a dozen entries in it.

"Okay, guys, I've been DYING to tell you this! You'll never believe how I actually found my diary! It's a very long and complicated story."

I took a deep breath and quickly rehashed everything, including how MacKenzie had sabotaged my Miss Know-It-All column by writing nasty letters to students and how she had posted her OWN bug video on the Internet. All to get me expelled for cyberbullying.

Chloe and Zoey shook their heads in disbelief.

"I think we should report MACKENZIE for cyberbullying!" Chloe said angrily.

"Yeah, I agree," Zoey added. "We can't let her get

away with this! You should tell Principal Winston and Mr. Zimmerman ASAP. Otherwise, you could end up looking like the guilty person and get suspended from school."

"Well, if I tell Mr. Zimmerman, I can kiss the newspaper good-bye!" I groaned. "He already threatened to FIRE me if I compromised the security of the Miss Know-It-All website."

"But you DIDN'T compromise its security!" Chloe asserted. "Your diary was STOLEN!"

"And it wasn't your FAULT!" Zoey insisted. "You're the VICTIM here!"

"Maybe. But STILL! They'd NEVER believe me!" I argued. "How can I convince them that MacKenzie is responsible for sabotaging my Miss Know-It-All site when she doesn't even attend this school anymore? I have no proof WHATSOEVER!"

"Sure you do!" Chloe smiled wickedly. "And it's in MacKenzie's OWN handwriting!"

"That's right!" Zoey agreed excitedly. "Your DIARY is all the proof you need!"

"Okay, guys, let me get this straight!" I said, trying not to freak out. "I'm supposed to just hand over my diary, which is filled with my deepest feelings, darkest secrets, and most embarrassing moments?! To Principal Winston and Mr. Zimmerman?! As evidence against MacKenzie?!"

"YES!" Chloe and Zoey answered emphatically.

"It's the ONLY way we can stop her!" Chloe argued.

"And the ONLY way you can protect YOURSELF from being expelled for cyberbullying!" Zoey reasoned.

"ARE YOU BOTH INSANE?!" I screamed at my BFFs. "Sorry, but I can't just turn over my DIARY to school officials. There's way too much personal stuff in there!!"

"Yes, I know it's going to be a bit embarrassing, but it's for the greater GOOD!" Zoey claimed.

"Just do the responsible thing and protect students from the real cyberbully—MacKenzie!" Chloe exclaimed.

"But what if it backfires and I get in TROUBLE for all the things I wrote about in my diary?!"

"Come on, Nikki, how bad can it be?!" Zoey asked.

"Well, I wrote that I thought Mr. Zimmerman was crazy!"

"Yeah, Mr. Zimmerman is pretty wacky!" Zoey snickered. "But I'm sure he can take a little joke."

"And even if he gets mad at you, so what?" Chloe giggled.

"And remember that time Principal Winston was eyeballing us at lunch and we started texting each other? I wrote all of that in my diary too! That Principal Winston would never believe we secretly hung out in the janitor's closet. Which, according to our school handbook, is an unauthorized entry by a student and a three-day detention for each occurrence!"

That's when Chloe and Zoey stopped laughing. Their eyes got big as saucers.

WHAT?!!!!!

My BFFs suddenly looked kind of worried.

"Actually, there's more," I continued. "I also wrote stuff about you guys. Chloe, you said we didn't look like people who would make prank calls from the library phone! And, Zoey, you said we definitely didn't look like students who would sneak into the boys' locker room! I also mentioned how the three of us snuck out of the cafeteria without any passes. That's at least FOUR school rules we've broken, some of them multiple times! But as long as you guys don't mind Principal Winston reading all of that stuff, then FINE! I'll report MacKenzie and turn in my diary as proof."

"OMG, Nikki! You wrote all the things WE did in your diary TOO?!" Zoey screeched.

"SORRY!" I answered sheepishly.

"ARE YOU KIDDING ME?!" Chloe shrieked. "We're looking at YEARS of detention! Our classmates will be seniors in high school and WE'LL still be in eighth grade, serving DETENTION! Do you have any idea how EMBARRASSING that is going to be?!"

"Yeah, and isn't there a rule that after an excessive number of detentions, they just give up on you and KICK you out of school?!" Zoey groaned.

"Sorry, Nikki, but there's NO WAY you can hand over your diary to Principal Winston!" Chloe ranted.

"Totally BAD idea!" Zoey fumed.

"Now, wait a minute! Let me get this straight," I said, narrowing my eyes at my BFFs. "What about the greater good and being responsible? NOW you're saying I CAN'T turn in my diary just because it has a pile of DIRT on you guys?!!"

"EXACTLY!!" Chloe and Zoey answered, glaring at me.

"I'm really disappointed in you two," I complained. "What do you have to say for yourselves?!"

"We're DOOMED!!" Chloe moaned.

"Our lives are SO over!" Zoey groaned.

At least we were FINALLY in complete agreement:
Seeking help from Principal Winston and Mr. Zimmerman
was NOT an option.

If they read my diary, there was a really good
chance my BFFs and I could end up in as much
trouble as MacKenzie!

YIKES!! ☹!!

"Listen, guys, maybe we're worrying for no reason,"
I said. "As long as MacKenzie doesn't make a move,
we won't need my diary, right? And by now she's
probably in Paris working on a report on the Eiffel
Tower with her posh new friends from North
Hampton Hills International Academy."

"Yeah, but didn't she say something about you
getting a surprise on Monday, April 20?! Well,

that's TODAY! And after stealing your diary and breaking into your website, she's capable of ANYTHING!" Zoey said.

Chloe tapped her chin, deep in thought. "Now, if I were a crazy, jealous, spoiled, high-strung, rich drama queen like MacKenzie, what would I do to get revenge?! Hmm . . . ?!"

"Well, to be honest, I've been really worried that she somehow sabotaged my advice column before she left," I explained. "But as soon as I found out what she'd done, I immediately changed my password so she couldn't log in to my Miss Know-It-All account anymore. And this morning I deleted ALL of her letters and checked everything AGAIN since my advice column is scheduled to publish in the newspaper today during lunch. My new website has this cool auto-publish feature. I just place my advice letters in a special file and they'll publish on a date in the future. But now that I think about it, I FORGOT to check that file."

Suddenly a little light bulb went off in my brain. That's when I totally panicked, and shrieked . . .

"Maybe THAT'S the surprise!" Zoey exclaimed. "What time does the newspaper publish today?"

We all checked the time.

"At 12:30 p.m.!" I said. "Which is in exactly . . ."

"FIVE MINUTES?!!!!" we screamed in horror.

Chloe, Zoey, and I scrambled for the door like we were on our way to a five-alarm fire.

"I'm going to my locker to get my laptop so we can log on to Miss Know-It-All to search for MacKenzie's letters," I yelled over my shoulder. "Could you guys stop by the newspaper office and grab my red folder out of my mailbox? It has hard copies of her letters. Then I'll meet you in the library."

"Okay. But hurry! PLEASE!" Zoey pleaded. "If MacKenzie's letters publish in the school newspaper and you're accused of cyberbullying and forced to hand over your DIARY to Principal Winston . . ."

314

"WE'RE DEAD MEAT!!" Chloe muttered.

It was actually a good thing MacKenzie transferred to a new school! Because if she hadn't . . . I swear! SHE'D be dead meat! That's just how ANGRY we were at her right then.

MacKenzie had left a ticking TIME BOMB at our school in the form of her Miss Know-It-All responses.

And now we had to find the bomb and defuse it before it EXPLODED!!

☹!!

When I left off, my BFFs and I were totally SPAZZING OUT over MacKenzie's letters.

That girl has done a lot of HORRIBLE things, but THIS stunt was the WORST!

Not only were her prank letters going to HURT a lot of innocent students, but there was a chance WE could end up EXPELLED from school! ☹!!

By the time we met back at the library, we had less than three minutes to find all MacKenzie's letters and remove them before the newspaper published at 12:30 p.m.

As Chloe and Zoey read over the printed copy of each letter and gave me details, I searched for it in my April 28 auto-publish file and quickly deleted it.

We were so stressed out, we were sweating bullets. I was typing as fast as my little fingers would go. . . .

ME AND MY BFFS, TRYING TO FIND AND
DELETE MACKENZIE'S LETTERS BEFORE
THEY PUBLISH IN THE NEWSPAPER!!

The good news was that we'd finally made it down to the last TWO letters ☺!! But the bad news was that we had less than thirty seconds to find and delete them ☹!! The situation was HOPELESS!

That's when Chloe said, "Remember, Nikki! If you fail, Brandon and this entire school could be reading your diary next week! So stay focused!"

"Thank you for reminding me, Chloe! But now I feel like throwing up!!" I muttered.

Zoey did a countdown like she was mission control for a NASA rocket launch. "Ten. Nine. Eight. Seven. Six. Five. Four. Three. Two. One! And we have publication of Miss Know-It-All!"

Then my BFFs waited anxiously for me to tell them the fate of those last two letters.

I sighed and gave them my saddest puppy-dog eyes, and their faces fell in disappointment.

It was so quiet, you could hear a pin drop.

Then I screamed . . . "WE DID IT!!" and my BFFs went BANANAS!!

YES! Somehow we'd managed to delete all of MacKenzie's letters seconds before the column posted! We were so happy, we did a group hug.

I was SUPERsurprised when I got a text:

"Chloe and Zoey just crashed the newspaper office and ran off with a folder from your mailbox. Is everything okay? BTW, does Chloe have BRACES?"

It was from Brandon ☺! And since he was actually texting me for the first time in WEEKS, it appeared he wasn't mad at me anymore. SQUEEEE ☺!! I was still pretty ticked off at MacKenzie for torturing Chloe like that. So I replied:

"Everything's fine. And yes, Chloe has braces! But before MacKenzie left, she traumatized the poor girl by cruelly teasing her."

I was SUPERsurprised when minutes later Brandon rushed into the library with a photo. He said it was a little present for Chloe that he hoped would make her feel better. . . .

CHLOE, FREAKING OUT OVER THE
SIXTH-GRADE PHOTO THAT BRANDON
FOUND OF MACKENZIE HOLLISTER

OMG! Apparently, MacKenzie's "perfect pearly whites" hadn't always been SO, um, PERFECT!! ...

SIXTH-GRADE PHOTO OF
MACKENZIE WITH BRACES?!!

"Why would MacKenzie say all those nasty things about ME wearing braces, when she had them too?!" Chloe exclaimed. "Go figure!"

"Probably because people who go out of their way to make others feel MISERABLE are SUPERinsecure and miserable THEMSELVES!" Zoey explained.

Chloe and I agreed. Soon the bell rang, signaling that lunch was ending and classes would be starting in five minutes.

We couldn't resist gossiping about MacKenzie's braces as we gathered up our stuff.

"Um, Nikki, can we talk for a minute?" Brandon asked, and kind of blushed.

I couldn't believe that Chloe and Zoey were clowning around and making kissy faces behind Brandon's back. They are SO immature!

I was going to DIE of embarrassment if he turned around and caught them doing that!

As soon as Chloe and Zoey left, Brandon pulled up a chair. But I was so nervous that I totally forgot to sit in a chair. Instead, I plopped my behind right on top of the table like an idiot and stared right into his beautiful brown eyes.

Brandon nervously brushed his shaggy bangs out of his eyes and then gave me a big smile.

Of course I blushed and smiled at him. Then he blushed and smiled back at me. All of this blushing and smiling went on, like, FOREVER!!

"Actually, I just wanted to thank you for helping me out with that . . . um, banana peel situation yesterday. And I wanted to apologize for not accepting your . . . um, apology."

"Well, I owe YOU an apology for not accepting YOUR apology too!" I gushed, and batted my eyelashes at him all flirty-like.

"I meant everything I said in my letter, Nikki."

"Really? Well, I'm really glad you wrote it. Even though it got stolen by a crazy drama queen and went missing for three days!" I blushed.

"Anyway, I wanted to talk to you alone because I'm thinking about asking this very special girl to hang out with me. But after everything that has happened, I'm really worried that she might say no. What do you think?"

Okay, that's when I got REALLY ticked off and thought, WHY is this dude even bothering to talk to ME if he is CRUSHING on some OTHER girl?!

Hey, what am I? Chopped liver?!

And then he has the NERVE to ask ME for advice on his LOVE LIFE?! Like, WHO does that?!

I couldn't help wondering if the girl was MacKenzie. Brandon probably thought she was SUPERcool now that she went to that really fancy school.

"Brandon, if she likes you, WHY would she say no?" I asked quietly.

NOT that I really cared ☹!!

Then he brushed his bangs out of his eyes and shot me a megawatt smile. But, personally, I didn't see what was so ding-dang funny.

"So, Nikki, would you like to hang out after school on Wednesday?" he asked, staring right into the murky depths of my tortured soul.

OMG! When he asked me that, I was SUPERshocked and surprised.

And happy! SQUEEE ☺!!!

Of course I said YES! The whole thing was SO romantic!!

That's when I noticed my BFFs were standing right outside the door with their faces pressed against the window, shamelessly SPYING on Brandon and me. . . .

BRANDON, ASKING ME TO HANG OUT
WITH HIM (WHILE CHLOE AND ZOEY
SHAMELESSLY SPY ON US) ☺!!

The good news is that it looks like Brandon and I are finally friends again.

SQUEEEEEE !!

And thanks to my BFFs, I managed to THWART yet another one of MacKenzie's evil, twisted, diabolical plans!

Even though MacKenzie has been gone for almost a week, she has somehow managed to create more DRAMA in my life than when she was physically present at WCD!

Thank goodness everything worked out just fine with my BFFs, my CRUSH, and my advice column.

Starting today, I plan to start living a happy, stress-free, drama-free, MACKENZIE-FREE life!

☺!!

WEDNESDAY, APRIL 30

Losing a diary can be pretty TRAUMATIC!

It almost feels like you've lost a piece of YOURSELF.

Believe me, I know from experience.

I really wanted to tell MacKenzie that I'd found ~~MY~~ HER diary when it accidentally fell out of her moving box that day she left.

I also wanted to encourage her to get a diary of her own and to continue writing in it.

Because sometimes a diary can help you vent frustration, face your fears, find your courage, embrace your dreams, and learn to love yourself.

And it's always better to rip into a page than another human being.

But most important, I wanted to tell MacKenzie

that I FORGIVE her for everything she's done to me in the past few weeks.

Because OMG! She's WAAAAAAAAAAY more MESSED UP than I am ☺!!

I'm just SUPERhappy to have FINALLY gotten my DIARY back!

SQUEEEEEE ☺!!

And I'm lucky to have the BEST FRIENDS ever!

We'll be hanging out after school today to celebrate our friendship.

SQUEEEEE ☺!!

Sorry, MacKenzie!!

In spite of your beauty, popularity, wealth, and killer wardrobe, I wouldn't want to be you.

Why?

Because, um . . .

I'm SUCH a DORK!!
YAY ME!!
☺!!

What does Mackenzie have up her
designer sleeves?

And why is her FAVE lip gloss color
Ready-for-Revenge Red?

Find out in . . .

Book 10

COMING SOON!

Do you have the whole DORK DIARIES series?
Collect all the adorkable books by Rachel Renée Russell!

Dork Diaries

Dork Diaries: Party Time

Dork Diaries: Pop Star

Dork Diaries: Skating Sensation

Dork Diaries: Dear Dork

Dork Diaries: Holiday Heartbreak

Dork Diaries: TV Star

Dork Diaries: Once Upon a Dork

Dork Diaries: How to Dork Your Diary

Dork Diaries: OMG! All About Me Diary

Double Dork Diaries

Double Dork Diaries #2

Double Dork Diaries #3

Ever wanted your very own Dork Diary?

Then look out for this special dork-tastic journal filled with questions from Nikki for you to answer across the year. Includes a squeee-worthy sticker sheet too!

Perfect for Dork fans everywhere!

ISBN 978-1-4711-2347-4

TIP 1:
DISCOVER YOUR DIARY IDENTITY

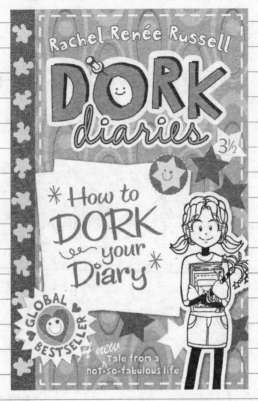

OMG, my worst nightmare came true—
I lost my diary!!
Chloe and Zoey are helping me search,
so I'm going to help YOU by sharing all of my tips
on how to keep a Dorky Diary!

more dorky fun!

Now you can find DORK DIARIES on Facebook and twitter too!

connect with other fans of the series!

Rachel Renée Russell is an attorney who prefers writing tween books to legal briefs. (Mainly because books are a lot more fun and pajamas and bunny slippers aren't allowed in court.)

She has raised two daughters and lived to tell about it. Her hobbies include growing purple flowers and doing totally useless crafts (like, for example, making a microwave oven out of Popsicle sticks, glue, and glitter). Rachel lives in northern Virginia with a spoiled pet Yorkie who terrorizes her daily by climbing on top of a computer cabinet and pelting her with stuffed animals while she writes. And, yes, Rachel considers herself a total Dork.